Thomas Adolphus Trollope

Leonora Casaloni

A Novel: Vol. I.

Thomas Adolphus Trollope

Leonora Casaloni
A Novel: Vol. I.

ISBN/EAN: 9783337045227

Printed in Europe, USA, Canada, Australia, Japan

Cover: Foto ©Andreas Hilbeck / pixelio.de

More available books at **www.hansebooks.com**

LEONORA CASALONI.

A Novel.

BY T. A. TROLLOPE.

IN TWO VOLUMES.
VOL. I.

LONDON:
CHAPMAN AND HALL, 193, PICCADILLY.
1868.

CONTENTS.

BOOK I.

A JOURNEY TO ROME AND ITS CONSEQUENCES.

BOOK II.

IN THE MAREMMA.

CHAPTER V.

CHAPTER VI.

CHAPTER VII.

CHAPTER VIII.

CHAPTER IX.

BOOK III.

FAMILY POLITICS.

CHAPTER I.

CHAPTER II.

CHAPTER III.

LEONORA CASALONI.

BOOK I.

A JOURNEY TO ROME AND ITS CONSEQUENCES.

CHAPTER I.

TALAMONE.

IT was a lovely evening about the middle of April; just the time of which the Italian poet sings, in words which may often be heard warbled from the mouth of *contadina* maiden, or making night musical in the stronger tenor of some youngster strolling homeward from the theatre through the moonlight streets,

"Come è gentile la notte a mezzo d'Aprile!"

How beautiful, in truth, is a mid-April night in the land of beauty of every kind; beautiful even in

the morne Maremma, where two or three months
more will make the beauty of the night full of
danger to any who may be rash enough to wander
beneath the stars for the enjoying of it !

But in April the beauty of that wild Maremma
land may be enjoyed without danger, and even the
nights are not yet poisonous.   It is a strange
country, that Maremma; outlawed, it might seem,
by both man and nature !   Or at least it was so at
the period of the events I am about to relate—some
forty years ago or so, that is.   Since that time
much has been done for the sanitary improvement
of the district, and more towards the redemption of
it from its old and well-known character of lawless-
ness and savagery.   Outlawed by nature, however, the Maremma could only be called in the
sense of its unfitness for human habitation.   For
it was, and is still, a district of exceeding beauty,
—a beauty ministered to by the very elements and
conditions which render its atmosphere pestilential
in the summer and autumn months.

Maremma is but short for *Marittima*, and desig-
nates the land by the sea—the *maritime* district
which stretches along the coast all the way from
Leghorn southwards towards and beyond Civita

Vecchia. It was not a shunned and banned region once. It is studded with the mighty ruins of Etruscan cities, whose colossal walls still serve to testify that an abundant and flourishing population once inhabited these now desolate hills and valleys. Hills and valleys is a phrase correctly describing the entire region. Englishmen, when they hear of a district infested by malaria, are apt to picture to themselves the wide flats of a fenny country, like those portions of our own island which are, in a modified degree, subject to the same misfortune. But nothing can be more unlike the Tuscan and Roman Maremma. The northern portion of the tract of country so called is known as the Tuscan, and the more southern portion as the Roman Maremma. The characteristics of the scenery in both parts are much the same;—a world of rolling hills—green in the spring with a thousand varieties of shrub: laurel, laurestinus, holly, citysus, box, arbutus in great quantity, dwarfed oak, and stunted ilex, with many another; gorgeous in the early summer with a wealth of colouring, among which the wonderful abundance of the scarlet arbutus-berries is the most prominent feature; and drearily brown in autumn — is intersected by a labyrinth

of small and generally exquisitely picturesque valleys, in the narrow depths of which, especially
where they near the sea, the Malaria witch brews
the poison which every landward breeze carries over
the hills and throughout the entire region. But
whether in spring, in summer, or in autumn, an
inexpressible air of morne desolation is over it all!
The human habitations, as may be imagined, are
few and far between; and the scanty inhabitants,
who brave the perils of the region, have impressed
on them, only too legibly, in face and form, mien
and bearing, the mark of the curse to which they
are doomed. It is not that the land is unfertile;
rich and heavy crops might be raised in those valleys
reeking with fever and ague; and in some cases rich
crops are so raised; but the cultivation is carried on
at the risk of life, and with the certainty of destroyed
health; and for the most part the men and women
who sow and reap these lands run from them to
some healthier place of refuge as soon as ever the
necessary labour has been done. But the inhabitants
of the Maremma are, or it may be more correct to
say, were, some forty or fifty years ago, recruited by
a contingent of a different class. It was, as has
been said, a lawless district. Things were done in

the Maremma, of which the law took little heed, which would have made other districts too hot for the doers of them. It was for the most part, too, a safe asylum for those who had done that which had made other parts of the country too hot for them. For the murderer or the hunted robber—in some cases for the political proscript — the tangled thickets of almost impenetrable thorn-bushes, or the covert afforded by the Titanic ruins of Etruscan walls, situated in some cases in the depths of pathless forests, afforded a safe place of refuge, and an unmolested home.

If it be asked how it has come to pass that this ill-starred region, which was once—from a thousand to two thousand years ago, perhaps—the thickly inhabited territory of many large and prosperous cities, has now come to be a type of desolation, shunned by man, and cursed by Nature, it must be answered that the change has been produced by long absence of all that care of man's hand which is needed to make earth fit for his habitation. The earth was given to man for his abode on the condition of subduing it, and holding it in subjection by the sweat of his brow and the skill of his brain. Left to itself, earth hastens back to its unredeemed

state of unbeneficent wilderness: and in this
Maremma region special causes have been at work
to make neglect especially fatal. Many small
streams, all but dry in summer, swollen torrents
in winter and spring, find their way to the neighbouring sea among these hills. But these torrents
come down from a part of the Apennine, the easily
disintegrated and friable soil of which is carried
away in large quantities by the waters when swollen
by heavy rain. The earth thus torn from the
mountains is carried by the streams as long as their
course is of a sufficiently torrent-like kind to give
a great impetus to the waters. But as soon as
they reach the more level portion of their course,
in the immediate neighbourhood of the sea, they
slacken their speed, and throw down their burden
to the bottom of their channels. Thus their free
exit to the sea is impeded. Pools and stagnant
lakes are formed, in which the mingled fresh waters
and sea waters are exposed to the action of a
terribly powerful sun; and it would seem that
mingled fresh and sea water thus acted on, have
the unfortunate property of producing a malaria
far more poisonous than would result from even
stagnant masses of either element unmingled with

the other. Thus it is that Nature revenges man's neglect.

In the southern part of the Tuscan Maremma, on the coast, at the extremity of a promontory facing southwards, in such sort as to form a deep bay, of which the general coast-line furnishes the other enclosing side, there is the town and port of Talamone. The port of Talamone! What memories and long-forgotten sweet classic rhythms are awakened in the mind by the word! Now the port looks as if the galley that carried Æneas might well have been the last that ever entered it! The port is scarcely so to be called now; and the town as little deserves the name which courtesy, shown to the memory of what once was, assigns to it. Among all the desolation of the Maremma, there is scarcely to be found a more desolate-looking spot. Decayed, squalid, dilapidated human dwellings have a physiognomy which speaks an abomination of desolation, more abhorrent to the heart of man than any mere absence of all signs of man and his works can do.

A few poverty-stricken fishers still own some half-a-dozen half-rotten boats, which seem to spend a much larger portion of their time rotting on the

sandy beach in the sunshine, which blisters and
bleaches them, than in the water. And these, such
as they are, lie not in what was once the port, now
utterly choked up by sand and mud, the accumulation of many a century, but on the beach at some
little distance from it. Yet the material aspect of
the scene is one of very great beauty; and there is,
especially at eventide, a melancholy character about
it, which seems to harmonise singularly with the
moral and social aspect of all around.

The coast-line, after jutting out to the southwards, and sharply retiring to the north again, so
as to form the promontory that has been spoken
of, at the extremity of which Talamone is situated,
resumes its southward course with a curve, and
trends away in a long concave line of low sandy
beach towards the foot of the Monte Argentario,
some ten miles to the southward. Having reached
the foot of that lofty mass, which, standing out
very boldly from the general coast-line, forms almost
an island, the coast becomes high, cliff-like, and
bold. The long low curving line of coast, which
thus extends from Talamone to the port of Monte
Argentario, may be said, for the greater and southern
part of the distance, to be not the real coast, inas-

much as it is merely a low line of sand-hills, behind which is a large extent of shallow salt water, made into a lake by another similar accumulation of sand to the southward of the mountain, which but for these two connecting sand-lines would be entirely an island. The wide shallow lake is thus shut in between what may be termed the real coast, the mass of Monte Argentario, and these two natural dykes of sand, one to the south of it, and the other to the north. They are very low; but yet that which forms the visible coast-line to the south of Talamone, is sufficiently high to prevent the ugly lake from being visible from that distance.

In the midst of this so-formed lake stands the little town of Orbetello, communicating with the main-land by a spit of natural soil, at the extreme point of which it is built, and with the Monte Argentario by an artificial causeway. Strange as it may seem, this little town so situated in the midst of its salt lake, is, though not by any means free from malaria, yet much less scourged by it than many other localities of the neighbourhood.

The Monte Argentario thus immediately faces Talamone; and a very magnificent object it is, rising to the height of a very considerable moun-

tain, whose craggy, and for the most part wooded
sides, are bathed by the bluest of bright blue
Mediterranean waters. Far to the west of it rises
from out these gently sleeping waters the Island of
the Lily,—the *Isola del Giglio*,—too far from the
Talamone shore for the eye to distinguish the mingled woodland and crag-land nature of its steep
sides, but near enough to contribute largely to the
beauty of the scene by the shifting and rapidly
varied effects of colour, light, and shade produced as
the sun gloriously sets behind it.

It was the hour at which Italians, whether on
the door-steps of narrow city alleys, or by wood-side,
or field-side, or sea-side, so dearly love to come
forth from the covering of roofs, and enjoy the
sweet influences of their delicious air and of the
evening hour,—the hour of the Ave Maria,—the
dear " ventiquattro," at which all toil ceases, and all
the world may lawfully give itself to enjoyment.
It seemed an hour which the still and melancholy
Maremma might in a special manner claim as its
own. The silent shores, the silent hills, the silent
woods, gathered a special and expressive beauty
from the lights peculiar to the dying hour of the
day. Even the squalor of the miserable little town,

burrowing in the sand, seemed glorified into a semblance of beauty, or at least of harmony, with the
other elements of the scene. But the outlook from
the coast seaward was gorgeously and magnificently
beautiful. The sun was falling into the western
blue in unmitigated splendour; and the golden
pathway through the darkening blue of the waters
came up from the far west like an angel's path,
straight to the spot on the shore on which two
women were sitting. A little behind, and to the
right hand of them, was what is called the town,
and every pane of glass remaining in the western
windows of it seemed a strongly burning fire,
under the painting of the level rays. The entire
outline of the western Island of the Lily was traced
in burnished gold against a purple sky. And all
the woods and crags of the nearer Monte Argentario
were bathed in light of every hue, from delicate
bloom like the pink of a rose, to deepest indigo,
warning that the glory was quickly passing away.

CHAPTER II.

BY THE SEA-SHORE.

THE two women, of whom I have spoken, sat on
a huge stone imbedded in the sand of the beach. It
was not a natural rock;—there are none such on
that part of the coast;—but a stone that had been
shaped by the hand of a builder, for what purpose
or how long ago, who shall say? It was, perhaps,
the sole remaining fragment of some pier, which
the Trojan exiles may have sighted from their
galleys as they followed their exploring way along
the coast, built when the neighbouring walls of
Etruscan Ansedonia enclosed a living city instead of
the wild boar's covert as now they do! Or it
may have been a portion of some coast fortification
of the Spaniards, of a date some two thousand years
later! There it is, built into the sand, with the

remains of a huge rusty iron staple bedded into one corner of it. The people of Talamone assuredly never ask themselves how or why or when it came there. It is natural to them to live among nameless and voiceless fragments of dead and gone civilisations! Huge cyclopic walls,—vast foundations laid deeper far than any modern spade has cared to follow them, and now meaningless,—half-ruined towers standing solitary and purposeless in the midst of wide uncultivated fields or thick woods,—these are to the denizens of the Maremma manifestations of the general course of this world's affairs, as normal as the setting of the sun, or the falling of the leaf, or the autumnal visitation of fever.

The two women sat on the ancient stone side by side, and gazed out seaward. They were not looking for any coming, or for any seaborne thing living or dead. They were simply gazing at the scene before their eyes; not consciously rendering to their own minds any account of its rare beauty; and still less remarking on any feature of it in spoken words. But none the less were they under the influence of it, and vaguely conscious of the enjoyment arising from the contemplation of it, and from the combinations of impression and sen-

.sation which resulted from the specialities of the place and the hour.

"The holy Virgin knows what will come of it!" said the younger of the two women with a sigh; "I went round by the *Madonna delle Grazie*, as I came in, and put up a couple of candles, and said the whole rosary twice through! God grant that it turn to good!"

"I don't know whether I would go with him if I was in your place, and you not a month out of bed since your child was born," said her older companion.

"I am well enough able to go. There will be no great hardship in the journey, for that matter. We shall travel with old Santi the *procaccia* as far as Civita Vecchia; and from there to Rome Sandro will find some of the *vetturini* that have brought down *forestieri* to Civita going back home. There are plenty of them, and Sandro knows a many of them," replied the first speaker.

"Oh yes! I don't doubt me you'll travel comfortable enough for that matter," returned the elder woman; "that's easy enough, I reckon, when there's money in the pocket. But I wonder you can bear to leave your own child, Lucia;—you who

have lost one—two—three children," she added,
holding up one finger after another,—"and that
too to go and bring home a stranger to take its
place!"

"No, not that! *Dio ne guardi!* God forbid!
And you are not to think, Giuditta, but what I
would give one of my fingers off my hand, that there
was no question of going to Rome, or that this
business had never been heard of! Santa Madonna!
that I would!—any finger but that," she added,
singling, as her hand lay in her lap, the finger
which bore her marriage-ring; "but Sandro says
it must be so, and—and—you don't know, Giuditta,
—but God and the Virgin know, that there is
nothing—nothing I would not do, if it were only to
get a smile from him!"

"And where did he first hear anything about
it?" asked the woman she called Giuditta.

"How should I know? I don't know whose
child it is—how should I? I don't know whether
Sandro knows himself! He says that there is
money to be got by it; and that I don't know
how hard money is to come by, and—and—that it
must be done!"

"Pretty money! that's to be the price of sacri-

ficing your own child. Bless the pretty dear little
face of it ! " said Giuditta.

"I wish it had been a boy!" said the mother,
musingly, and gazing out into far distance along
the path of gold, which the rays of the setting
sun were making across the blue waters,—gazing
with those eyes that seem to be looking into the
far future rather than at any materially visible
object in space. "I wish it had been a boy, for
Sandro would have liked it better, and perhaps——"

Two large silent tears welled out from the large,
liquid, mournful eyes that had once contributed
powerfully to make the speaker's face a very lovely
one, and might have made it seem so still to eyes
which could appreciate form and expression more
than the freshness of merely animal beauty. Two
tears rolled slowly down the pale sunken cheeks
of delicate clearness and purity of complexion, apparently unnoticed by her in the abstraction of her
mind, busy with the far-off "what might have
been ! "

"Nonsense! Have liked it better! What would
he have better than a blessed infant that promises
to grow into beauty with every day it lives? You

mark me, Lucia, if that child don't live to be a beauty one of these days! And suppose you can't suckle 'em both?" asked Giuditta suddenly, after a pause.

"Then we shall send the strange child to the Innocenti at Florence!" said the mother with prompt energy. "Oh! that is quite settled. Sandro says that if I find, when the child is here, that I cannot manage with both, he will send the other child away. He has promised me that. But I dare say I shall be able to keep 'em both, without one doing a bit of harm to the other."

"But why shouldn't you take the little one with you on your journey?" inquired Giuditta.

"I wish I might, with all my heart. Santa Madonna! I wish I might! But Sandro will not let me. He says I shall be back the second day; and that, properly cared for, the child can take no harm in that time. You will take care of her, Giuditta! I know you will care for her!" said the poor mother.

"Never you fear for that, Lucia, *mia poveretta!* I'll care for the child as if she were twice over my own. How came you to call her Stella, instead of your own name, Lucia?" asked Guiditta.

"Stella was my mother's name; and two of the children I lost were baptized Lucia. I would not try the name again!" said the mother, with a long quivering sigh.

"Well, Stella is a good name. I like Stella— Stella! Look at that big shining one that has just come out over the mountain there, a little to this side. Little Stella will grow to be as lovely and as bright as that is!"

"Then you will come up to our house early to-morrow morning;—we shall be starting early;—or better still, if you could come back with me to-night. You could have half my bed, you know. Sandro won't be at home till to-morrow morning, a little before it is time to start," said Lucia, again sighing deeply.

"Who has got the child now?" said Giuditta.

"Old Marta Fosti. She looked in coming back from the town, and I begged her to take the little one a bit, while I came down to speak to you. She'll want to be going home, old Marta; and I must be going too, for I have kept her long enough."

"Well, I will go with you to-night, *Lucia mia!* It will be better than coming to take the child all in a hurry to-morrow morning. You will have time to tell me anything about the little one. And then you'll be having a bit of something when you get home; and, to tell the truth, I haven't so much as a crust in the house, or a *quattrino* in my pocket!"

"Come along, then. Yes, there is bread and a bit of *salame*, and a flask of wine, in the house; and you are more than welcome, *mia buona* Giuditta. Let's go, and lock your own door, and be going up the hill."

And the two women rose from their seat accordingly.

It was visible as she rose, that the younger woman, whom her friend had called Lucia, must have possessed also, besides great beauty of face, a tall, finely formed, and even elegant figure. But there was now an air of suffering and a faded appearance, which were at present more markedly characteristic of her person. It was not that there was any symptom of hard poverty about her appearance. Her dress was of a superior kind to that of her friend Giuditta. And there was no appearance, notwithstanding what Giuditta had said of the state of her finances, and of the emptiness of the cupboard at home, that she either was suffering

from any very severe degree of poverty. She was
a bony, square-built woman, rather under the
middle height, the robust strength of whose constitution seemed to have given her an immunity
from the normal attacks of fever and ague, which
had left their marks on nearly every man and woman
of the population. She was decently and comfortably dressed in a short petticoat of blue serge,
with a gay-coloured little shawl, folded cornerwise,
over her back and shoulders, so worn as to let her
arms, clad in clean but coarse white cloth spun from
hempen yarn, come freely out from beneath it. On
her head she wore nothing but her own abundant
black hair, now streaked with grey. Giuditta
Fermi was the widow of a man who had kept a small
attempt at a mercer's shop in the town of Talamone,
and she now maintained herself as best she might
by acting as a tailoress for male or female customers
indiscriminately; often, in the case of her country
patrons, going to their house and staying there to
do what had to be done in the way of mending up
the habiliments of the family, and remaining there
till the job was done. She thus managed to " *buscare
la vita*," as an Italian would say, without suffering
from any of the severer ills of poverty, though it

often occurred to her to be sore in need of some little assistance, which it had often been in the power of Lucia Vallardi—that was her friend's name—to give.

Lucia was the wife of Alessandro, or Sandro Vallardi, and they lived in a lone house amid the woods, on the high ground of the promontory at the point of which Talamone is situated. What Sandro Vallardi was it would not be easy to state so simply and straightforwardly as has been done with reference to Signora Giuditta Fermi and her late husband. To tell what he had been would involve a longer story than can conveniently be told here on the threshold of another story, with which his antecedents had but small and indirect connection. He was a man evidently of superior education—to use the ordinary phrase—to that of the peasants and fishermen who lived around him. But it might be gathered, even from so much of him and his life as was patent to the observation of the very small little world in which his home-life was passed, that whatever that education had been, the moral results of it could not be said to make him the superior of the more ignorant boors who almost exclusively made up that world.

In a word, it was tolerably well known in that little remote and isolated world that the occupations of Sandro Vallardi were such as put him at odds with the laws of the other big world which lived away under happier skies than theirs, in Florence, in Leghorn, or Sienna. And it was still more clear, though the house in which he occasionally, and his wife Lucia constantly, lived, was his own, together with the three or four acres of almost uncultivated land around it, yet that no miracle of highest agricultural care and success could extract thence the means of subsistence, and of that degree of comparative ease of circumstances which characterised the Vallardi household, as contrasted with that of the other inhabitants. But nobody cared to make any inquiries, or even conjectures, on this subject. It was one of those many matters which an Italian man's nature and breeding and traditional habits teach him are better not known or inquired into. What was the good of knowing? Perhaps inquiry or spying might lead to knowledge which might at some day or other turn out to be very inconvenient. Who could say? Suppose those troublers of life, the lawyers, should one day or other come asking questions, how much better and pleasanter to be able to say at once, with a safe conscience, that they knew nothing!—the answer which every Italian would always fain give to any legal, magisterial, or police inquiry.

Nor did the vague general notion of the nature of the affairs in which Signor Sandro Vallardi might be supposed to occupy himself during his long and frequent absences from home, at all tend to produce any feeling of dislike or reprobation in the minds of the people around him. Who would not pitch lawyers, and tribunals, and courts, with all their rules, and exactions, and botherations, and taxes, to the devil, if they could and dared? Surely he who waged war against all this must be regarded as an exceptionally fine fellow, as long as he did so successfully, and must be entitled to commiseration and compassion if it should come to pass that in the long run the unequal struggle should go against him.

And then Vallardi looked like a fine fellow, a great point with all people, and especially so with the southern nature of the Italians. He was a man of some forty years of age, tall and muscular, with a handsome face, abundant black beard, moustaches, and whiskers, a large dark eye deep sunken under a somewhat forbidding, but still handsome

brow, a straight nose, white teeth, and a complexion of cheeks, throat, and neck as deep-red a
brown as quickly circulating blood, and plenty of it,
and habitual exposure to sun and every sort of
weather, could make it. How could such a man—
especially when clothed in a laced black velveteen
carniera, or large jacket, a high black felt hat,
leather breeches, and gaiters showing a well-made
leg—be otherwise than a fine fellow, and clearly in
the right in any differences he might have with
odious law and lawyers?

Lucia had deemed him a fine fellow,—the finest
she had ever known, at the time when she first
saw him,—and had accordingly given him, as his
by right divine, all she had to give, her heart
and herself. There is nothing unusual or surprising
in that. But it may appear so to those who knew
something of their reciprocal relations since, and
nothing of a woman's heart, that her opinion on
the subject still remained well-nigh unchanged. She
had discovered, indeed, with infinite heartbreak and
unending self-reproach, that she was not, as she
had once hoped she might have been, a due and
fitting mate for one so highly gifted;—that her
poverty of nature and unworthiness had failed to

retain his love. But her own love and admiration for the man, who had been, and was still for her, the embodiment of her conception of the heroic, was unchanged and unchangeable. He was still her beau-ideal, her master, her lord, her god! His smallest meed of approbation was the highest bliss to which she aspired;—his most transient smile her happiness for a day!

It was an unquestioning, unchangeable, animal-like devotion;—a devotion of that kind which most men think one of the most beautiful spectacles the world can offer; and which most women therefore profess to think beautiful also. Certainly poor Lucia, in the blindness of her fetichism, the rich overflowing of her love, the fulness of her loving heart, commends herself to our pitying love. But I cannot think her error beautiful, though it is tragic. I do not like or admire real tragedies. I think that if the Fates had willed to put our poor Lucia in her youth through a course of Euclid and conic sections, she would have been less likely to make a fatal mistake and wreck herself upon it.

Is it a latent consciousness of this truth that makes most of the master-sex so averse to "unfeminising" the female mind by any such discipline?

CHAPTER III.

There is perhaps no spot in all Rome which appeals more forcibly to the imagination by its associations, or to the eye by its special beauty, than the open space at the west front of the Lateran. It can hardly be that any visitor to the Eternal City can have forgotten it. Behind him who stands on the broad platform bounded by the three or four large shallow stone steps, which raise it above the level of the surrounding turf, is the mother church of Christendom. St. Peter's, with all its magnificence, is but (historically and morally considered) the rank fungus growth of a period when the causes which had begun to sap the strength of the Church, and which are working, and will work its ruin, were already in existence;—a period, too, when the golden age of architecture had already passed away. The purely ecclesiastical associations connected with the gorgeous fabric are all disastrous, and belong to a period of decline and debasement. The very style of its architecture speaks of church degeneration. Not so is it with the venerable structure of the Lateran! And surely if there be any building in the world, the history of which must make it venerable in the eyes of Christians of every mode of faith, it must be this! Every stone of the ancient pile is instinct with memories of the times when Mother Church was still a civilising and beneficent agent, and had not yet become the bane and enemy of humanity. Every form and detail of ornamentation carries the mind back to the best ages of architectural art.

Standing thus before those venerable portals, the eye sweeps with its gaze the whole of the hill ranges which shut in the Campagna to the south. And surely for mere material beauty there is not such another range of hills on earth! Across the melancholy Campagna, dumb with the terrible oppression of its countless memories pressed down into its silent bosom by the weight of layer over layer of successive civilisations vanished, stretches still with

giant strides the mighty line of arches which were
raised by the people who dwelt on the soil and
possessed it before Christ was born! On the right
hand of one standing as I have supposed, there is
close under the city wall one of the prettiest grave-
yards in the world,—the Protestant burying-place,
with the great pyramid tomb of one who was neither
Catholic nor Protestant towering above the modern
tomblets lying at its feet. Close in front of the
gazer is the old Porta di San Giovanni, through
which some picturesque sample of the picturesque
Roman life is sure to be passing; one of those
quaint wine-carts, with its little triangular perch
of skins and boughs arranged to protect the driver
from the sunshine; or a flock of goats, with their
four or five buskined goatherds, hardly less shaggy
and wild-looking than the animals they are driving.

In short, it would be difficult to name a spot
where all the specialities which go to make Rome
unique among the cities of the world, are combined
with so happy and perfect an effect as that wild-
looking bit of open ground before the west front
of the Lateran Basilica.

It is again eventide on the third day after that
on which Lucia Vallardi and Giuditta Fermi con-

versed on the shore near Talamone. It is again
the hour of the Ave Maria; and the sun is gilding
the mountains to the south of the Campagna with
hues as gorgeous as those he lent on that evening
to the Isola del Giglio and the Monte Argentario.
Close at the foot of the old wall which encloses a
portion of the collegiate buildings of the Lateran,
and forms a right angle with the west front of the
church to the right hand of it, a group of three
figures is sitting on the turf, listlessly, to all appearance, enjoying the pleasantness of the evening hour.
They sit by preference in the small space of shade
cast by the wall; for, though it is still April, the
sun has begun to have considerable power, and his
level rays darted full against the front of the church,
are more scorching than an Italian, always cautious
of exposing himself to the heat of a spring sun,
would needlessly affront. The group of persons in
question are nearly the only living beings visible in
the wide space between the church and the city gate,
which equally take their name from St. John.
Nearly so; not quite. There is a small country
cart, drawn by a pair of dove-coloured oxen—huge,
gaunt, wild-looking beasts, with thin flanks and
huge ribs, very visible under the loose hide, and

colossal horns—and its driver in slouched hat and
shaggy sheepskin coat, slowly approaching the city
gate, on its homeward way to some farm in the
Campagna.   And there are three or four lazy
officials of the gate lounging their seedy lives away
under the shadow of its roof.   But this is at a considerable distance from the church, and from the
spot where the above-mentioned group is sitting,
and, prowling as they are under the deep shadow of
the gateway, they are hardly visible.   There is a
solitary goat browsing under the wall which stretches
from the gate in the direction of the Protestant
Cemetery ; and there is an old sacristan, but half
alive apparently, standing at the western door of
the southern aisle of the church, to which he has
crawled from some inner recesses of the huge pile,
to enjoy—he, too—for a few minutes the evening
air, and to look once again on the glorious prospect
of mountain, plain, ruined tower and crumbling
arch, which he had looked on daily for more than
half a century, while still they changed not, save
with the changing light of the changing seasons.

No other life was breathing in all that wide
extent.   And very soon there was no longer even
that.   The " sweet hour of gloaming " is nowhere

sweeter than in Italy; but it is very short. If it is
brighter than under more northern skies, its flitting
must be, as the song says, "still the fleetest!" No
sooner has the last limb of the sun disappeared
behind the rim of the horizon in these southern latitudes than it is night. And your Roman, even in
April, loves not the dews of the hour which follows
the sunset. The old sacristan has retired from his
brief airing, and has closed the heavy portal behind
him with a hollow sound, re-echoed from the lofty
wall under which the group of three were sitting,
which seemed the knell of yet another day gathered
to the tomb of its predecessors. The peasant and
his oxen have passed out of the gate; and the denizens of it have cowered in beneath the shelter of
their dens in the thickness of the old walls; a little
urchin has emerged from some hole in ruined wall
or tower, and has led away homewards his friend
and companion the solitary goat; and it is night, and
all is silent as the grave.

Still the three persons sitting at the foot of the
wall do not move from their position. Apparently
they are heedless of the Roman dews; but it is
hardly likely that they are continuing to sit there
for the sake of enjoyment. They are, to all appear-

ance, waiting; and the time or the person for whom
they are waiting has not yet come.   Twice the deep-
toned bell of the church has tolled out the quarter
of an hour, and the little knot of three—two men
and a woman—have remained impassably sitting in
the same position at the foot of the wall.

At last a figure emerges from the darkness round
the south-western corner of the church, and advances
into the open flagged space in front of the building.
It is comparatively light there; for the flagstones
are white, and there is no building to intercept the
little light that still comes out of the western sky.
The figure—a long, slender, dark figure, with a singularly unbroken column-like outline—comes slowly
towards the middle of the church front, and pauses
there to look peeringly around him.   At the same
time the three sitters rise from the ground, and
move, not towards the new comer still standing in
the midst of the open flagged space, but a little
way along the foot of the wall.   Their movement
has attracted, as they had intended, the attention of
the figure in front of the church, and he comes
towards them, slowly, and with apparent caution.

It is a tall young man, evidently, from his dress,
a seminarist, or some such aspirant to the ecclesias-

tical career, on whom Rome sets her mark from the very early years of childhood. The young man in question, however, must have been nearly, if not quite, of years to receive his first orders; and he may perhaps have been a sub-deacon. Doubtless any one properly instructed in such matters would have known at once, from some speciality of his costume, whether such was the case or not. To the uninitiated, the question was doubtful. He was clothed in a long, black, close-fitting, and perfectly straight-cut garment of the cassock kind, which reached from his neck to his heels, and gave him, as he stepped slowly across the open space, the appearance of a black moving column. His arms were held up in front of his breast, and, as he neared those he was apparently seeking, it could be seen that he carried something in them; but the burden, like all else about him, was black, and the nature of it therefore undistinguishable.

When he had come near enough to the wall under which the two men and the woman had been sitting to be within the shadow which still made it a little darker there than in the open part of the ground, the three who had been waiting advanced to meet him. And one of the men, a fine, stalwart figure,

above the ordinary height—Sandro Vallardi, as the
reader has already doubtless divined—stepped out a
pace in advance of the others, and said to the young
ecclesiastic :—

"Are you seeking one from the Tuscan Maremma,
signore?"

"Si, signore," returned the young man; "I am
sent here to seek a man and a woman, who come
from that part of the country."

"We come thence, signore," returned Vallardi.

"But you are three. My instructions were that
I was to meet one man and one woman," rejoined
the young figure, who still held his burden, covered
with a black shawl, close to his person.

"I am the man and this is the woman!" said
Vallardi, indicating his wife with his hand. "This
young man," he continued, pointing to the third of
the party, who hung a little behind his companions,
"is merely a servant of mine, whom I have brought
with me in case my wife might need any more
attendance on the journey than I could give her.
What you have in charge to bring me—under that
black shawl there—is something to be entrusted to a
woman rather than to a man, is it not? That may
satisfy you that you are speaking to the right person."

"Oh! it is no doubt all right. Besides, my orders are not to ask questions, but to deliver this child to those whom I should find here awaiting it. You are prepared to receive a child, signore, are you not?" said the young man.

"I should like, however, to make sure that there is no mistake, by hearing from you the name of the person who sends the child. If it is that of my friend and correspondent, then I shall be sure that it is all right. It will be more satisfactory," said Vallardi.

"My instructions were, as I have said, signore, to ask no questions, and they were also to answer none," said the young ecclesiastic impatiently. "I was told, indeed, that none would be asked me," he added.

"Very well. So be it. Caution is good in these things, doubtless; and doubtless, too, it is all right. My wife is ready to receive the child," said Vallardi.

Lucia advanced a step as her husband spoke; and the young seminarist, or deacon—whichever he may have been—removed the black shawl which covered the child he had been holding in his arms, and placed it, fast asleep, in a large and warm wrapper which Lucia had brought with her for the purpose of receiving it. She received the child in silence, wrapped it carefully, and held it to her bosom.

"I have to tell you, further," said the young ecclesiastic, "that the child is a female, that it has been baptized; you may name it, however, as you will. I have no further orders." And so saying he turned on his heel, and recrossed the open flagged space in front of the church, towards the south-western corner, round which he had come, without once looking behind him.

If he had done so, he would have seen the third member of the little party from the Maremma stealthily following him; or rather, probably, even if he had turned to look, he would have become aware of nothing of the sort. For "Il Gufone,"—the big owl,—which was the *soubriquet* by which Signor Vallardi's follower was known among his friends, was a masterly hand at the execution of such a commission as that wherewith he was now entrusted; and for the performance of which he had been expressly brought from Talamone. He would have found no difficulty in tracking a more experienced and difficult quarry than the young ecclesiastic from one end of Rome to the other. When Vallardi had asked for the name of the sender of the child, he had not expected that his question would be answered. It cost nothing to try; and it was possible that some bit of information might have been gleaned from the reply. But he had brought Il Gufone with him to Rome, for the express purpose of dogging the steps of the person who should bring the infant, and thus discovering who the parties were who consigned the child he had undertaken to receive to his keeping.

Vallardi stood still and silent for a minute or two, watching the stealthy progress of Il Gufone across the pavement, and till he vanished round the south-western corner of the church, with a smile. Then turning quickly to his wife, who was trying to see by the faint light of the stars, now peeping forth, what the child she had received was like, he said, as he, too, turned to quit the open space—

"Come; come along! put up the brat. You will have time enough to look at it; more than enough. Come along, or Gamba will think we are not coming to-night."

"How far have we to walk?" asked Lucia.

"How far? To the gate, of course; the gate for Civita. One would think the woman was a fool! Don't you know that Gamba has to go to Civita to-night, and is waiting for us outside the gate?" said Vallardi, as he walked on with a quick stride.

"I did not know it, Sandro," replied his wife meekly; "you never told me."

"I suppose you thought that you were going to stay at Rome for the rest of your days. But that would not quite suit."

"I am quite contented to go back to Talamone, Sandro. I am sure I had rather be where you are, than anywhere else in the world—let it be Rome, or anywhere else," said the poor wife.

"But I am not at Talamone very often, or am like to be much. But come, let's get on. You'll go better if you save your breath, and don't chatter."

The husband and wife left the open space, passing round the same corner of the church by which the young ecclesiastic, with Il Gufone at his heels, had preceded them. But they neither of them perceived that they also were followed in their turn.

Near to the west door of the northern aisle of the great church there is a large buttress jutting out some four or five feet, in such a manner as to throw the corner behind it into very deep shadow. From this dark nook a slight figure darted forth, just at the same moment as Sandro and Lucia Vallardi passed round the opposite corner of the church.

It was the figure of a young lad, of some fifteen years old or thereabouts, dressed like the son of a well-to-do farmer; a light, lithe, active figure, barefooted, though no other part of his costume seemed to indicate poverty.

He flitted across the wide front of the church with the agility and noiselessness of a squirrel, and succeeded with little difficulty in tracking Vallardi and his wife through the streets of Rome till they came to the gate leading towards Civita Vecchia. There he came up with them, and passed the gate at the same time, remarking to Vallardi in passing that he was all behindhand, and must make the best of his way to his father's farm, three miles from the gate. Thus saying, he set off running along the road, while Gamba, the *vetturino*, was taking the corn-bags from his horse's mouth, and Sandro and Lucia were taking their places in the carriage. But as soon as he had reached a spot in the road out of sight from the gate, he stopped, hid himself behind a hedge, and when the *vettura* passed, jumped up behind it, and there remained till it neared the station for its halt and the baiting of the horses. Then skulking by in the dark, he repeated the same process when the carriage again overtook him, and arrived at Civita Vecchia at the same time with his

unconscious fellow-travellers. And he started with
them again, or rather a little behind them, when
they left Civita Vecchia at a little after noon on the
following day. The pace at which the *procaccia*
travelled on the hilly Maremma road, along the
coast between Civita Vecchia and Orbetello, the
place to which he was bound, was not such as to
try the powers of a less active courier than he who
was tracking the course of Signor Sandro, severely.
There were frequent halts for refreshment of man
and beast, and for the execution of commissions
along the line of road. The active barefoot little
peasant of the Campagna kept up with his quarry
with very little difficulty, and never lost sight of
them till he had fairly seen them housed in Signor
Vallardi's house on the wild hill-side on the wooded
promontory above Talamone.

He then quietly, and with cautious care not to be
seen till he was close to the more inhabited part of
the country, struck across the woods and fields in
the direction of Orbetello, there, apparently being
sufficiently supplied with money, obtained refreshment and rest, and on the following day made the
best of his way back to Rome.

What he did as soon as he arrived there, will be
een in due time.

CHAPTER IV.

GUFONE'S REPORT.

SANDRO VALLARDI remained at home after his return from Rome for a longer time than he had ever done for very many months before. Nor was he during this time specially surly or brutal to his wife. And poor Lucia almost began to dare hope that better days than the past might yet be in store for her. Something of the old light came back into her eye; and at times, when a gleam of hope that Sandro still loved her, crossed her mind, a delicate shade of rose-colour would slightly flush her clear and transparent cheek, and show her, to any eyes that could appreciate beauty of a pale and delicate cast, to be still a very handsome woman.

It very soon began, however, to be evident that Lucia would not be able to give nourishment to both

her own little Stella, and to Leonora at the same
time. She confessed this inability to her husband
with fear and trembling, dreading that it would be
the occasion of an outburst of anger and violence.
But he bore the disappointment, if such it were, with
moderation, and told her if she would try it a little
longer, only till Il Gufone should return from Rome,
the necessary step for relieving her should be taken.

Il Gufone had been longer absent than Vallardi
had expected. Nevertheless he waited patiently at
home, rarely leaving the house, except to stroll up
the hill with a gun over his shoulder, till the second
night after their return from Rome. And on that
evening, while Sandro was smoking his cigar after
supper, and Lucia was dividing her cares as best she
might between the two claimants on them, the door
of the house was opened, and Il Gufone made his
appearance.

As seen in the darkness of the evening, under the
shade of the Lateran, there was little to remark
about him beyond the general appearance of lightness
and agility, joined to a slender and somewhat under-
sized figure. As he entered the light of the large
room,—hall, kitchen, and eating-room, all in one,—
in which Vallardi and his wife were sitting, the

peculiarities of Il Gufone's appearance might have attracted more observation. The wide and lofty room which occupied the greater part of the ground-floor of the house, and was, indeed, the only portion of that floor used for purposes of living in, was lighted, not only nor chiefly by the one tall brass oil lamp, which was burning on the table, but by a blazing fire of huge long faggots burning in an enormous hearth. For it was in the Maremma. And though at Rome it might be desirable to seek shelter from the rays of the April setting sun, on the hill above Talamone it was both more comfortable, and wiser in a sanitary point of view, to cheer the April night with a good roaring fire, the materials for which were to be had in any plenty for the cutting, within ten paces of the door.

As Il Gufone, entering with the manner of one who was no stranger, either to the place or the people in it, came forward into the light of the blazing fire, I have said the appearance of him was a somewhat peculiar one. He had an immense head, made to look still bigger by the dishevelled condition of his elf-like shock bush of hair,—hair of a very different sort from such as we are wont, erroneously, to consider as the invariable product of Italian blood.

Nanni, or Giovanni, Scocco,—for such were the
baptismal and ancestral names which Il Gufone kept
for use on high and solemn occasions,—was undeniably Italian in every sense of the word. And
Titian, though he was not wont to select exactly
such types as Il Gufone for the subjects of his brush,
has left to us abundant proofs that hair exactly of
the tint of his was in that day not unfrequently to
be seen on the heads of high-born Italian beauties.
It is not, perhaps, so common among either the
men or women belonging to the lower grades in the
social scale. But as for the inheritance of blood,
who knows, for that matter, by what paths, or
through what channels it passes? Assuredly Nanni
Scocco himself could have thrown but little light
on the genealogical question as to the parentage
from which his profusion of auburn red hair of the
true Titian tint had descended to him. The features,
above which it tossed and tumbled about in a huge
tangled bush, could not certainly be said to be of the
type usually intended to be designated by the term,
aristocratic. The tint of them, however, was not of
the ordinary Italian plebeian swarthiness. His face
was white, but it was not the whiteness, also common
in Italy, that often goes with dark hair,—the

whiteness which the French call *mate ;*—but a sickly, unwholesome-looking hue, better described by the unpleasant epithet, cadaverous. He had large, wide-opened, blue eyes,—very beautiful eyes in any other head, but hideous in that of poor Nanni, for one of them was placed very perceptibly higher in his face than the other, and they were bordered by inflamed, red lids, that had not the effect of showing them to advantage. Beneath them was a broad, flat nose, and a monstrously huge mouth, with thick, out-turned lips, and a mighty range of large, powerful, and brilliantly white teeth. His huge head was placed, without any intervening neck, on a pair of very broad, muscular shoulders. And the arms that came from those shoulders were out of all proportion, long ; and the great, bony hands at the end of them out of all proportion, large. But all the rest of his body seemed to taper away into flimsiness. The legs were long for the trunk, but small, and by no means straight.

Yet, with all this, there was an air of great agility, and even of power and activity, about the figure. The queer, ill-shaped legs must have been all sinew and bone ; for they assuredly served their master better than many a handsome leg is capable of serving its owner.

Where and how he and Vallardi first came into
contact and relationship with each other, neither
Lucia nor anybody else about Talamone knew. One
day, some four or five years before the time here
spoken of, Vallardi had brought him home with him,
after one of his frequent absences, and he had ever
since been a sort of hanger on about the place in
some altogether indefinite capacity. Vallardi in
speaking to the stranger in Rome, had called him
his " servant ; " but this was only " per far figura,"
as an Italian so often says ;—a little bit of swagger,
merely adopted for the moment, as suited to the
occasion. Certainly no relationship of master and
servant existed between Vallardi and Nanni Scocco,
if the payment and receipt of wages be deemed an
essential part of such a connection. Mostly, Vallardi,
when going on those expeditions which took him so
frequently from home for weeks or more at a time,
used to take Il Gufone with him. Sometimes he was
left at Talamone ; and whether Vallardi were at
home or not, Nanni always had shelter, and as much
as he chose to consume of whatever food was going.

As soon as Vallardi saw the grotesque figure of
his henchman coming from the darkness around
the door into the fire-light, he snatched a plate

from the supper table at his elbow, and flung it
with all his force at the big red head which gleamed
in the light. Il Gufone dodged his head aside
with a perfectly self-possessed mastery of the
situation. The plate was shivered into pieces against
the further wall of the big room; and Nanni in
the same instant sprung with one bound to the
corner of the long table nearest to him, and seized
by the neck one of the large Tuscan wine flasks,
which hold three ordinary-sized bottles, with the
very evident intention of hurling it at his patron's
head, in return for the salutation with which he had
been welcomed. But he was not so prompt in his
anger as his elder and superior; and having grasped
his weapon, hesitated.

"Ay, do, do! you mis-shapen spawn of the devil!
I think I see you at it! Ay! a worm will turn,
they say; but I never saw one that could bite.
Bah! *imbecille!* Don't you see; there's wine in
the flask? You'd better drink it, with an *accidente*
to you; for if you throw it away, devil a drop more
will you get to-night!"

Lucia, meantime, at the first semblance of the
outbreak of a row, had gathered up her two babies,
and scuttled away to the foot of the stairs, which

opened on a far part of the room, and escaped to
an upper chamber.

Il Gufone, thinking discretion the better part of
valour, and struck by the practical value of his
patron's concluding suggestion, took the hint, and
quietly poured himself out a large tumblerful of the
red wine,—black wine, as the Italians more generally call it,—and drank it off.

"There! Now perhaps you will tell me why
you have kept me waiting here two whole days for
you, you idle vagabond! Unless another drink
would make your ugly shock head any the clearer!
Where the devil have you been, you blinking
gufo?"

Again Il Gufone judged it desirable to accept
the suggestion thrown out to him, and re-filled and
re-emptied his tumbler before attempting any reply.

"There!" said Vallardi again, as the young man
set down his glass, "now you can speak, I suppose,
now that you have soaked the lump of ashes you
call your body enough to make it hold together a
little longer! Where have you been?"

"Lump of ashes yourself!" retorted Nanni;
"I'll hold together when you're gone to dust, never
fear! Lump of ashes! There's very few specimens

of the best flesh and blood, see you, that would carry themselves from Rome here in the time I've taken to do it ! "

" What have you been about, then, I should like to know ? " grumbled Vallardi, glaring at him.

" Why what I generally am about—doing what you bade me, worse luck to me ! What the devil else had I to do, or where else had I to go to ? Do you think I should have come back here, if I had ? "

" I think you had better not have done anything else, if you care about holding together a little longer, as you say. But now for your report. Have you found out what I want to know ? "

" Yes, I have ! And if you know of anybody who could have done it quicker, I wish you'd send them upon your errands another time, I do, you tyrannical, insolent, ignorant, malicious, stupid old scoundrel ! " said Nanni, grinning at him and screaming a crescendo emphasis upon each succeeding epithet.

" There, you'll feel better now ! " said Vallardi quietly and cheerfully, as if the storm had served to clear *his* mental horizon also ; " now let's hear, without more ado, what you have to tell me."

" Well ! " said Nanni more quietly, as if he did

feel all the more able to tell his story for having thus relieved his mind, " I followed the young fellow, priest or whatever he was,—*che so io !*—to a far-off part of the city on the other side of the Tiber. That was not difficult; for he went along without ever looking back, as if he had the devil behind him."

" Natural enough," said Vallardi.

Il Gufone acknowledged the complimentary insinuation only by a grin, and went on with his report.

" But he went to a house that did not seem likely to be such an one as I was in search of;—a poor tumble-down old place, inhabited by a lot of poor devils;—not the sort of folks who want to get rid of their children, or any way who can pay people well for ridding them of them. I found out easily enough that it was the home of the young fellow's mother. So there was no more to be done that night. He did not come out again."

" You did not show yourself in making inquiry, I suppose ? Because, *amico mio*, somehow or other people when they have seen you once, are apt to know you again," sneered Vallardi.

" I swear by all the Saints," replied Nanni, " that

one would think you imagined me to have no more
brains in my head than you have! No! nobody in
the house saw me! I found out all I wanted to
know from a boy in the street, not much handsomer,
and not much stupider than myself. Ah! I know
the look of the heads that have got brains in them.
They don't look like your's, Signor Sandro!"

"Very good! If you belong to the brain family,
I must be of a different blood. All right. Go on
with your story, Gufone," said Vallardi quietly.

"Well, the next morning I was watching, and
the young fellow came out early, about seven
o'clock, dressed just the same as the night before,
and away he goes, douce and quiet, with his eyes on
the pavement all the way, till he came to a big
palace out by the church of Santa Maria Maggiore,
and in he goes, and walks straight up the stairs
without speaking a word to the porter, though there
was a porter, as big as—pretty nearly as big as
you, Signor Sandro, and I should think near about
as clever by the look of him—standing there at
the door of his den under the archway. The young
'un was at home there, and no mistake. That looked
more like it. Well, it was easy enough to find out
that that was the Palazzo Casaloni."

"Casaloni!" interrupted Vallardi, "why the great villa near San Salvadore, away there under Montamiata, belongs to the Casaloni!"

"And why shouldn't it? What in the name of all the Saints has that got to do with it? Well, you may have a fine black beard, Signor Sandro, but for anything behind it—if ever there *was* a *zuccone* for a head-piece!" sneered the Gufone with an expression of unmitigated contempt.

"All right! *amico mio!*" rejoined Vallardi with unruffled good humour. "If you had failed to find out what I told you to find out, I would have broken every bone in your ugly carcass. As you have found out, you shall have the reward of being as saucy as you like;—and I know that's what you like best in all the world, you crooked cantankerous cur! Go on!"

"Well, I say it was easy enough to find out that the *palazzo*, where the young priest marched up the great stairs in that way, was the Palazzo Casaloni. And then, as it happened, it was not much more difficult to discover who lived in it. For there is no part of it let to *forestieri*, or to anybody. Nobody lives there except—"

"Except the Marchese of course. Do you think

that the Marchese Adriano Casaloni was likely to let his *palazzo* to the *forestieri ?*" interrupted Vallardi.

Il Gufone nodded his great head three or four times at his patron before he answered him. "Yes! that is the sort of way you would pick up information, if you were to try to do it for yourself! Well, I do believe that I am not a beauty; but sooner than be such a handsome booby,—such a mere outside and case of a man,—as a body may say!— Well!—No! the Marchese Casaloni don't live there. Not a bit of it. He lives away at the villa under Montamiata, and never comes to Rome at all."

"Who the devil does live there then?" said Vallardi, with more show of impatience than he had exhibited during the foregoing part of the Gufone's narrative.

"Why, his brother, a bishop, I believe, or something of that sort. Any way, a 'Monsignore;' and he is a much greater man than the Marchese, his brother. And it took some little time to find out all about him, as you might understand, Signor Sandro, and some little brains, too. But that you can't understand. However, I did find out that he is a very great man at Court, and likely to be made a Cardinal; and I'll tell you what, Signor Sandro,

is the long and the short of it: as sure as I have
brains in my head and you have none in yours, the
child that the Signora Lucia carried up-stairs in a
fright just now—when you tried to cut my head
open by way of getting the quickest way at what
was inside it—is the child of Monsignore Casaloni;
and the reason why the child is sent away is that
he is terribly afraid that if any talk about it should
get abroad, and be heard at the Court, it might be
the means of spoiling his hope of being made Cardinal. All that I found out! Catch you finding it
out for yourself!"

"I prefer making you do it for me, thank you,
Gufone. You have done it so well that, besides being
as impertinent as you like, you shall have some
supper," said Vallardi.

"I should think I should too! Do you think
there would remain much to eat in the house if I
was told to go to bed supperless?" returned Nanni,
who was, however, no longer really in an ill-
humour.

"Perhaps not, if I were to suffer you to remain in
the house; but once outside you might howl round
the door like a wolf, only that a wolf could not look
half so ugly. I suppose you were not able to hear

anything about the mother of the brat?" he added, while Nanni prepared to avail himself of the permission that had been so graciously afforded him.

"Humph! I had no orders to do that," said the Gufone, with his big mouth full of bread and *salame*, or uncooked but well-smoked sausage, highly flavoured with garlic.

"No; that is true. All I want of anybody is to obey orders," replied his patron.

"Ah, yes! You'll do all the brain-work yourself, won't you? Just like all the other great captains, eh? That's just what they all say. But I'm thinking that few of 'em would *be* great captains if those they give their orders to didn't many times think for 'em," rejoined Nanni, who, having despatched his bread and *salame*, was now busily preparing a mess of cold haricot beans with vinegar and oil *à discretion* —a luxury which to a Tuscan peasant is equivalent to strong beer *à discretion* to Englishmen.

"Humph!" he grunted again, as he with gloating eye copiously anointed the plate before him piled with the soft flowery beans; "I wonder whether you would pitch another plate at my head if I was to tell you that I *did* find out something about the mother of the Monsignore's child?"

"Perhaps I might; I won't answer for myself,"
replied Vallardi composedly.

"Pitch away then and smash the crockery : it is
not mine! Only look out for what may come back
again !" snarled Nanni. "Well, then ;—yes, I did
find out something about the mother, for I thought it
might, may be, turn up useful," he added, after a
pause, during which the greater part of the well-oiled
beans had been shovelled into his huge mouth,
accompanied by great wads of bread saturated in
the oil which flooded the plate.

"Well, that depends—depends on many things,"
replied Vallardi thoughtfully ; "depends in the first
place on *what* it was that you found out."

"Well; I found out her name. She is the
Contessa Elena Terrarossa. She is a great lady,
too ; and it has always been kept very secret
that there ever was anything between her and
the Monsignore. That's what I found out !"
returned the Gufone, not without a manifestation
of justifiable pride.

"Oh ! that's what you found out ! Well, that
may turn out useful. But, I say, *Gufone mio*, how
about it's having been kept so very secret, if you
were able to come at the knowledge of it in a few

hours, eh?" said Vallardi, looking at his follower with one eye closed.

"Secret!" echoed the Gufo; "what's ever kept secret from such as I get my information from? Secret!—It's secret enough from the Pope, and the Cardinals, and the Bishops, and the Monsignori, and the Princes, and the Signoroni;—*accidente* to them all for a pack of old humbugs and fools! But do you think the sharp boy that does the porter's work for him, and minds the gate, and gives him a call when he is gone to the caffè round the corner, and gets a handkerchief full of broken victuals for his pains,—do you think he don't know all about it? Of course he does, being a sharp boy, with a shock-head and a wide mouth, may be, and not a fine black beard and a handsome-shaped empty skull behind it! Ah! there's plenty of people in Rome that know all the secrets that would make a pretty kick up if the grand folks, that think they know everything, were to hear them!"

"The Contessa Elena Terrarossa!" said Vallardi to himself thoughtfully. "I'll tell you what, Gufone," he added, after a considerable pause, "you have done your commission so well that you shall have still another reward, you shall have another commission—always on the same understanding, that I will break your bones for you if you fail to do it satisfactorily : you shall go back to Rome."

"*Accidente* to me if I go back to Rome before I have had a good four-and-twenty hours to rest —that is, unless I have money to pay for carriage hire," said Gufo, not altogether unreasonably.

"Come ; you shall have both—rest and money to pay the *procaccia*. You shall have to-night to sleep, and you shall go with the *procaccia* from Orbetello to-morrow. Of course you can't go riding into Rome as if you were a monsignore. You must find your own way through the gate. And what I want you to do is this :—Find out whether this child was sent away with the consent of its mother, the Contessa Elena, or whether it was done against her wish ; whether she would have wished to keep the child—the mothers of 'em mostly do, though it seems strange they should ; and see if you can learn at all what sort of a woman she is, this Contessa Elena Terrarossa ; whether she is rich or poor, handsome or ugly, young or old ;—you understand ? "

" If I didn't understand what you mean and what

you want better than you do yourself, Signor Sandro, it would be a pity. I'll find it out for you, you give me money enough to eat, and, may be, to treat another boy, while I am at it."

"All right, Gufo! And now you may stow away that hideous carcass of yours among the straw, and snore away till you wake in the morning!"

The poor Gufo was ready enough to do so, now that he had satisfied the more pressing need of supper, for he had travelled far that day and fast —farther and faster, as he would have been ready to boast, than many a man who looked able to beat him out of the field would have done.

Vallardi remained awhile in meditation over the embers of the abundant fire, made a note or two in a note-book he carried about him, and then followed his trusty henchman to rest.

CHAPTER V.

STELLA IS SENTENCED TO EXILE.

In accordance with the promise that had been made to him, Il Gufone was permitted to prolong his well-earned slumbers to a late hour on the follow ing morning. The *procaccia* was wont to leave Orbetello on his southward journey at four in the afternoon; and it would need about three hours for the Gufo to go to the little town from Vallardi's house. It would be sufficient if he started at about one o'clock. There was no need of saying any-thing more to him respecting the matter confided to him; so Vallardi let him sleep till he woke of his own accord about midday. There was a parting skirmish between the superior officer and his lieu-tenant, in the course of which it was arranged between them that the latter should be supplied with a sufficiency of money, not only to pay the *procaccia*, but to eat well all the time he was to be absent, with some small matter over for the treating of any comrade of his own order, whom, in the pursuit of the useful knowledge he was in quest of, it might seem desirable so to propitiate; and, on the other hand, that every bone in his skin was to be broken if he returned without the required information. These preliminaries duly settled, Il Gufone set out on his mission at the hour named, having just before starting carefully inserted a lucifer-match into a cigar, which Vallardi had put out of his hand for a moment, and seized an opportunity of skipping up-stairs into his patron's sleeping-room, for the purpose of hastily but neatly placing the frying-pan between the sheets of the bed.

When he was gone, Vallardi still gave no indication of any intention of immediately leaving home. But it was rarely that he remained there so long at one time as had recently been the case; and Lucia feared that he might go before she should have definitively made to him the communication which she so much dreaded, to the effect that she found it altogether impossible to retain both the babies, and should have obtained from him the per-

formance of his promise, that if such should be found
to be the case, the little stranger should be sent to the
Innocenti—the foundling hospital of Florence.

Vallardi turned back into the house from standing
before the door for a minute or two, while looking at
Nanni Scocco, as he wriggled, jumped, and shuffled,
rather than ran, down the path over the rough
ground which led from the house in the direction of
Talamone.

"What a devil's imp it is!" he said to his wife,
who was sitting by the ingle with one baby at her
bosom, while she rocked with her foot a cradle in
which the other was lying;—"a veritable imp of the
devil! But he has some brains in his head, as he is
so fond of boasting! He'll do the job I have
sent him on better than any other that I know of,
though he does look more like a wild animal than a
man!"

"Poor Gufone! he means well!" said Lucia,
sighing.

The sigh had no very intelligible reference to the
matter of her speech, but applied in poor Lucia's
mind to the general constitution of things. Life
was a melancholy affair to her; and she had a habit
of sighing, which sometimes singularly irritated her

husband, when she would fain have done aught that was within her power to please and propitiate him!

"Means well! Yes, very—as when he was going to throw the wine-flask at my head last night, if his courage had not failed him! But what the devil is there to sigh about it? Damned if you don't find matter for sighing in everything, let it be what it will! There's no blister like a regular discontented woman."

"I am never discontented, as long as I have you with me, Sandro!" pleaded the poor worn woman; "but it was not about Il Gufone I sighed. I was thinking of the children, and it vexed me to have to tell you that I can't manage to keep the two of them. I know you wish it, and I *am* so wishful, Sandro, to do always as you would have me."

"And, like the rest of you, you always talk about it most when you *don't* do as I would have you. But I am not one of those that can be put off with words instead of deeds. *Do* as I would have you, and I'll say, thank you! But it is not a bit of use talking to me about your being *wishful* to do it!" said her husband with a heavy scowl, as he stood with his back to the fire, and took up from the table the cigar which he had put out of his hand just before Il Gufone started, and into which that well-meaning young gentleman had found a spare moment to stick a lucifer-match. Vallardi proceeded to light his cigar, and received a puff of flame and sulphur in his face, which singed his moustache, and brought the water into his eyes.

"Cursed imp of hell!" he exclaimed, throwing the cigar into the fire; "one is never free from his damned idiot tricks! But one's wife thinks it is all very well-meaning! I wish to God the mischievous devil's imp was here now! I'd show him how well-meaning I feel towards him! I'll break his cursed misshapen bones for him as soon as I set eyes on him, and then you may sigh for *that* at your leisure, Signora Consorte!"

"But about the children, Sandro?" said Lucia, looking up at him timidly, after a pause.

"Damn the children, and you too! And you wonder that I am not fond of staying here more than I can help! Well, what about the children?"

"I was saying, Sandro, that with all the will in the world, I cannot manage to keep the two of them. They would both go to the bad, poor innocents! And for all you speak so, *Sandro mio*, I know you would be sorry that our little Stella should go like the others went."

And she shifted the child she held from one arm to the other, in order to put out the hand that was nearest to him, and try to take his as it hung by his side. It was a piteous, wan, very thin, blue-white hand, long and taper, which had been beautiful once, but which, as it was now, was of itself suffi-cient to tell a tale of sorrow and long-suffering. The handsome, stalwart man, in the perfection of health and strength, snatched his hand away with a frown and a shrug of his broad shoulders when he felt the touch of the cold frail fingers against his own, as if he had shrunk physically from contact with weakness and failing vitality.

"Could I help their dying?" he snarled savagely. "Was that my fault too? Any way *I* will take care that bad nursing shall not be the death of this one. She shall be sent where she shall be properly taken care of."

"What, little Leonora? That was what I was saying, husband. I would have kept the two of them, if I could; indeed I would."

"Oh, damn your whining! it's enough to put a man into his grave with the everlasting sound of it.

No, not little Leonora. That was not what *I* was saying. You say that you are afraid that you may lose your child now, as you have lost three before. I say, therefore, that it shall be sent where it is sure to be properly nursed. You will care less, I presume, about the other brat."

"Oh, Sandro!" cried the poor wife, looking up into his face, with her quivering white lips unclosed, and her large eyes wide opened with alarm; "you don't mean to send away our own little one, our little Stella? You mean the Roman child. You said it should be so, you know. You can't mean to send away our own little child! It is such a beautiful darling! It is your own image, Sandro! It has your own beautiful eyes! Neither of the others was like this! No, you didn't mean that, I know. I am stupid; and I know I don't always understand you."

"Ugh—h—h! what an inundation of words! A priest is nothing to a woman for palaver. Damn'd parcel of stuff. If you don't always understand me, see that you do now; and it shan't be my fault if you don't. Your child, Stella, shall be sent to the Innocenti at Florence, where it is sure to be properly taken care of. Do you understand that ? She may have my eyes, and beard too, if you like ; but she shall go to the Innocenti for all that. You will then be able to nurse the other child ; and if that dies in your hands as the other three did, it will not so much matter, you know."

Lucia for a few moments seemed to be struck dumb by this award of fate. Then she burst into violent weeping.

"Oh, Sandro, Sandro ! " she said amid her sobs, "dearest Sandro, my own husband, you will not take her from me. You will not take the child, your own child, away. You promised me, you know ; you promised me that the other child should be sent away if I could not nurse it. You know, Sandro, that you said it should be so ; and you always do as you say."

"When I said so, I did not know what I now know. What I do is for the advantage of all, yours and the child's above all. I know what I am about. As soon as Il Gufone comes back from Rome, the child will be sent to Florence," said Vallardi doggedly, though speaking with less violence than before.

"But I will try, Sandro ; let me try a little longer, and see whether I cannot keep them both. I cannot

part with my child, I cannot, Sandro. I will do as
you wished, I will keep them both. I beg your
forgiveness for saying that I could not. I will try."

" And the child will die, as the others died. Both
of them would die, most likely; and that would
not suit my book at all. No, it must be as I have
told you. You had better make up your mind to it
at once. As soon as Il Gufone comes back from
Rome, Stella must be sent to Florence. Why, you
foolish woman, she will be much better cared for
there than you can care for her; you, who have had
such bad luck with your other children. Now let
me have no more whining. I am going up the hill,
and shall not be back till supper-time. See that you
have made up your mind to take it quietly by that
time."

He turned to leave the house as he spoke, but
looked round as he reached the door, paused a moment, and then came back to the place where he had
been standing before the fire.

" And, by-the-bye," he said, " there is one other
thing which it may be as well to mention at once,
to prevent accidents. I mean that it shall be supposed here by all the damned fools who love to
meddle with what does not concern them, that the

child sent to the Innocenti is the stranger child
from Rome. You find that you are unable to nurse
the two, and therefore are obliged to send away the
nursling, which is a pity and vexes you, because the
money paid for the nursing of it is thus lost. Do
you understand?"

Lucia was rocking herself backwards and for-
wards in her chair in mute distress, and made no
answer.

"Do you hear me?" asked her husband roughly;
"and do you understand me? Answer, will you?"

"Yes, Sandro, I understand," said the poor
woman submissively.

"Take care then that you do not fail me in this,
if you care ever to see my face again. Let me see,"
he added after a pause, "who is there here who has
seen your child sufficiently to know that the other
child, which will remain here, is not yours?"

"Giuditta! Giuditta Fermi would know it. She
knows the blessed face of my darling, and would
never, never, mistake that dark thing for it," replied
the mother.

"Giuditta Fermi! Very well. It shall be
Giuditta who shall take the child to the Innocenti;
and I will take care that she holds her tongue."

"The Gufone would know too! He knows the difference between the children well enough," added Lucia, with a sort of eagerness that seemed as if she imagined that such a difficulty in the path might suffice to alter her husband's will.

"Bah! Il Gufone! As if he would ever dream of breathing to any human soul what *I* wish to be kept secret. Il Gufone will go to Florence with La Giuditta. She may be afraid to go alone with the child; and it will be better to have an eye on her. So now, then," he added, looking sternly and intently into his wife's face, while she looked up at him with the tears rolling down her thin sunken cheeks, "so now, then, this matter is settled. And I expect that you will never let me hear any word further on the subject, and never hereafter make any reference to the fact that it is your own child who has been sent to Florence instead of the stranger."

And with those words he turned on his heel, and left the house.

Lucia knew her husband well enough to be very sure that there was no shadow of hope remaining for her that the doom she had heard pronounced could be averted or changed. She knew also that it behoved her to be at least silent and acquiescent

when he should return in the evening. She took
her treasure in her arms, leaving the other child,
against which a sort of hatred seemed creeping into
her heart, sleeping in its cradle, and carried it
up to the upper chamber, and laid it on its back
on the pillow, and stood with her two thin hands
folded on her swelling bosom, gazing at it as if she
had brought it thither for the purpose of thus taking
her last look and last farewell. Then she knelt
down by the bedside and wept,—not hiding her sad
face, but still gazing,—gazing with, oh! such intent-
ness of wistfulness at the little creature, which gave
back smiles for her agonising tears. And thus she
remained till it was time to think of busying herself
in the preparation of her husband's supper.

Thus she prepared herself for obedience to the
commands she had received. And when Vallardi
came back at eventide, no further word was said as
to the fate destined for the little Stella.

CHAPTER VI.

A PLEASANT INVITATION TO SUPPER.

THE next day Vallardi strolled down the hill to
Talamone, and entered the dilapidated little tene-
ment in which La Fermi carried on her business
when she was not engaged at the houses of any of
her clients. He was fortunate enough to find her
at home as it chanced, but he did not deem the
sort of little shop, open to the street, in which he
found her, well adapted to the opening of the business
he had in hand. The surprise of La Giuditta, on
her part, was great at receiving the honour of such
a visit. It was a very common thing for the Signora
Lucia to come down and have a bit of chat, especially at times when her husband was absent, but La
Giuditta could not remember that Signor Vallardi
had ever done so before. La Giuditta, like most of

the other inhabitants of Talamone, mixed a certain
quantity of something rather akin to terror with the
admiration with which she and they regarded Signor
Sandro Vallardi.   And he seemed so large in her
little bit of a shop, and looked so magnificent in his
black velveteen jacket and scarlet sash round the
waist, that poor little Giuditta was almost too much
taken aback to speak the ordinary words of welcome
adapted to the occasion.

"I have a few words to say to you, Signora
Fermi," said Vallardi, not seeing, or not condescend-
ing to notice, her flutter of surprise; "but this
seems hardly a good place for the purpose.   I have
something to propose to you, in fact, which may be
advantageous to you ; and if you will do me the
favour to walk a little way up the hill with me, we
can talk better there than here."

" *Ma come !* with pleasure, *mio buon Signore !*   I
trust the Signora Lucia is well ?   I was afraid, to
tell the truth, when I saw you come in, that there
was something the matter with her."

"No, not she !   She is much as usual.   If you
like to come back with me, she will be glad to see
you, and, may be, she may have a word or two to
say on the matter in hand—women always do have

such a lot of talking to do!—and you could have
a bit of supper with us, and walk down the hill in
the evening."

All this was very singularly gracious from so
very fine a fellow as the great and rather terrible
Sandro Vallardi, and La Fermi felt not a little mys-
tified in attempting to guess what it might mean.
However, it was quite clear that there could be no
thought of anything but prompt compliance with so
gracious a mandate. And little Giuditta set off in
a sort of shuffling amble by the side of her magnificent cavalier, who strode along utterly regardless
of the poor little woman's difficulty in keeping up
with him.

"You know, I think, Signora," began Vallardi,
as soon as they were clear of the few houses which
still cluster round the spot where the fort once
was, and call themselves the town of Talamone,
" you know, I think, about the child that my wife
took in to nurse, eh ? "

"Si, Signor Sandro, I know. I was afraid that
two babies might be too much for her," replied La
Giuditta, beginning to guess that her services might
be required in some way for getting the stranger
child off her friend's hands.

"Ay! that is just it. You were very wise, Signora Giuditta. And it turns out just as you thought," said Vallardi, with a sort of inward smile to himself.

"Well, then, you must send the little stranger away, Signor Sandro; that's all about it. There's always the hospital for such things."

"Just so, Signora Giuditta; you are an understanding woman. But you see my poor wife has lost three children already, and I don't think she makes much of a hand at nursing. Now, at the Innocenti, the great hospital, you know, in Florence, they have the best nurses, and the best care that can be had for money. And that's what I want for my child. If it had not been for the luck of this child being sent to her to nurse, I should have been loath to take the child from her, for fear she might be solitary like, and fret over it. But now she will have little Leonora to nurse; and I mean to send our child to the Innocenti."

"What, send away your own child! Well "——— said Giuditta, interrupting herself, and judging it prudent to suppress the remainder of what she had been about to say with a sudden gulp.

"Why, what, in the name of all the saints, can I

do better for the child? If I leave it with the mother it will die, two to one, like the others. No, I will have better nursing for it than can be got here—the best of nursing!" said Vallardi, speaking with some degree of irritation, but striving all he could to suppress the appearance of it.

"Well, may be you are right, Signor Sandro. Everybody knows his own business best, and it's not for me to put my say in the matter," said Giuditta, bringing her conscience and her desire to propitiate her companion as much into accord as she could.

"Well, that is just what I say! Everybody knows his own business best; and I am doing the best I can. But I don't like to be interfered with by a parcel of fools—not sensible people like you, Signora Giuditta—who will meddle with what they have no concern with. I can't stand that. And I do not choose therefore that it should be known that I have sent Stella to the hospital. I mean to let it be supposed that it is the other child that has been sent to Florence."

"Ah—h—h!" said Giuditta, drawing a long breath.

"*You* know all about it, of course. And my wife

has that opinion of your judgment that I should not have liked to decide on it without consulting you. Therefore, as you see, I give you my confidence. But there is nobody else who will know the real truth. And I must tell you, Signora Giuditta, that if there is one thing more than another that I can't bear, it is having my confidence betrayed. That I consider the basest thing anybody can do. Why I declare, so help me God!" he said, raising his voice and stopping in his walk, while he faced round and looked at the little woman straight between the eyes with a terrible expression, "I declare, before all the saints, I should have no more scruple in putting a bullet through the head of anybody, man, woman, or child, who betrayed my confidence, than I should have in crushing that flower!" and he set his heel viciously upon a poor little anemone as he spoke.

Poor little Giuditta shook in her shoes as she saw and heard him.

"I should never think of betraying a confidence that was placed in me," she said at last in a shaking voice; "it is not my principle, and never was."

"Ah! I am so glad to hear that—very glad," said Vallardi, in a voice of great relief; "for what a sad thing it would be for me to be the death of such an old friend as you! But I should do it as sure as fate. I could not help myself. I could not, indeed, if I was to be betrayed. If ever you were to mention to any human being the fact that it is my child Stella that has been sent to the Innocenti, instead of the Roman child Leonora, I should shoot you through the head as sure as you stand there. I should just walk down one night, and kick the door of that old ramshackle place of yours off the hinges, and step up to your bedside, and do the job, without either one or two; but———" and he pulled out a pistol as he spoke, and made as if pulling the trigger of it close to little Giuditta's head, to her unspeakable terror. "But there is no fear of that happening," he continued, "for it's very easy for a body to hold her tongue, you know, Signora Giuditta."

"I shall never speak about any babies at all, or any hospital; that will be safest. I shall try not to think of any such things at all," said the poor little woman.

"Brava! I see we shall always be good friends. And now that we have settled that point for good and all, I must tell you that my wife wants you to

be so kind as to take the little one for her to
Florence. Of course you will be at no penny of
expense. You will travel comfortably. You will
get a visit to Florence—perhaps you never saw
Florence? You will have a look at it without
putting your hand in your pocket; and you will
only just have to carry the child to the tourniquet
at the hospital, and give it in to the person that
answers the bell. What do you say to it, eh,
Signora Giuditta?"

"Well, you know, Signore Sandro, I shall lose
more than one good job while I am away. I stand
engaged to go over to old Anna Piccardi, the *fattore's*
wife, at Tretorri, on Monday next; and I should
be at Caparbio the following Thursday. And it
stands to reason, you know, Signor Sandro, that a
poor woman like me can't afford to lose her work.
Seeing Florence is all very well for them that can
afford it, but a poor widow-woman like me has other
things to think of."

Vallardi smiled grimly at her as she heaped up,
with the readiness of the true Tuscan peasant, the
reasons which went to show that she ought to make
as much as possible out of the affair proposed to her.

"It is all very true, Signora Giuditta," he said,

" and of course you are right to make the best bargain you can. But if it costs too much, Lucia must go herself, and I and Gufone must do the best we can with the other brat till she comes back. But if a trifle of a couple of Francesconi or so, in addition to all expenses, would make it worth your while to undertake the job, why that should not stand in the way."

" *Faccia lei!* Settle it on your own terms," answered Giuditta in the usual formula of a Tuscan assenting to the conditions proposed to him, the idea in his mind being that it is as well, after having bargained for the uttermost penny to be got, to get also credit for obliging you in the matter. " For me," said the Signora Giuditta, " it is sufficient if I can render any service to you and the Signora Lucia."

" She will be very glad to have the advantage of sending the child under your care. There is only one other thing to be said," continued Vallardi, with the air of a man accustomed to make the wills of other people bend to his own ; " mothers don't like parting with their babies even for their own good, much as they profess to love 'em. That seems so selfish to me ! However, if Lucia should show

any unwillingness to send Stella to Florence,—
though she must know it is the only sure way to
save her life,—mind you don't encourage her. That
might make me very angry.   And somehow or
other, though really I am one of the most good-
natured, easy-going fellows alive, I am apt to get
very dangerous when I am made angry.   It is the
fault of those who make me angry.   Don't *you*
make me angry, Signora Giuditta.   We are such
good friends, it would be a pity.   So take care
you don't say anything to encourage Lucia to
think ill of sending the child.   You understand me,
eh, Signora Giuditta?" he concluded, again looking
at her with a glance that made her tremble.

"Si, signore ; I understand.   When do you intend
that I should go with the child, Signor Sandro ?"
she asked.

"As soon as ever Il Gufone comes home.   He
is gone upon an errand; and as I mean that he
shall go with you to Florence, we must wait for his
return ; but I expect that he will be here in a day
or two."

"Oh !—Il Gufone is to go to Florence with me
and the child?" said Giuditta in a rather doubtful
tone.

"Yes; that will be much better than going alone, you know. He will take care of you, and be of use to you on the journey. Shan't you be glad to have him with you?"

"Only—only that sometimes Il Gufone is apt to—to be mischievous in a way, as a body may say. He is such an one to play tricks," said poor Giuditta, who would far rather have been left to her own devices.

"Let me catch him playing tricks when he is trusted with an errand by me! He knows too well that I should break his neck for him. You need not be afraid of his tricks when I send him to take care of you. If I was to say, 'Gufone, worry the Signora Giuditta; I have a spite against her;'— ah! then indeed it is like enough that you might begin to find your life a burthen to you. But that is another matter. You will find him a very useful travelling companion, I assure you."

Signora Giuditta answered only by a passive sigh; and they walked on a little while, he striding up the hill, and she trotting in no very comfortable state of either mind or body by his side.

"I begin to be ready for my supper," said Vallardi, as they came near his place of abode, "and

I hope you are, Signora Giuditta. You won't be
sorry for it after your walk, eh?"

"No, Signor Sandro; I dare say I shall be glad
of a bit to eat when I get there. But now I feel
more out of breath like," panted the poor little
woman.

"What, you don't generally come up the hill so
fast, eh?" he answered with a grim smile. "Well,
we are nigh at home now. Remember all I have
said to you, Signora Giuditta, and we shall have a
very pleasant supper."

And with that he pushed open the door of his
house, and politely held it open for his visitor to
enter. They found the table prepared for supper;
but the large room was empty.

"Lucia!" cried Vallardi, going to the foot of the
stairs, "here is the Signora Giuditta come to sup
with you. Come down and let us have something
comfortable as quick as you can. The Signora
Giuditta has made me walk up the hill at such a
pace that I am as hungry as a priest after a twelve
o'clock mass."

He spoke in a tone that indicated to his wife's
practised ear that he was in high good humour,
and she hastened to come down the steep stair

from her evening crying, with pale face and lips
and swollen eyes, and a child in her arms, prepared
to look to the best of her power as nearly cheerful
as she had ever looked for many a long year.

" It is very good of you to come up to me, Giuditta. There is Leonora in the cradle up-stairs;
would you mind going up and bringing her down?
I will have the supper ready directly."

The little woman went on the errand assigned to
her with alacrity; and as soon as she had done so,
Lucia, with her own child still in her arms, was
about to go up-stairs again, as if for some need connected with the preparations for supper. But her
husband stopped her with peremptory voice and
gesture.

"No; one at a time up-stairs, if you please! If
you want anything up-stairs, you may go as soon as
she comes down,—not before."

His wife yielded at once without a word of reply,
and busied herself, as well as the burthen at her
breast would permit her, in getting the materials
of the supper placed upon the table.

"I have told her," continued he, with a toss of
his head towards the rafters of the room, intended
to indicate the person spoken of, "that she is to

take Stella to the Innocenti at Florence. She saw,
as any sensible woman would see with half an eye,
that it is the only way to give the child a chance. I
told her, too, that Il Gufone would go with her.
She did not seem half to like that; but I am not
going to trust her alone."

His wife said nothing; but looked at him with
a dull, heavy, imploring eye. But the meaning in
the look was sufficient to banish all Sandro's good
humour.

"Ah-h-h! let alone a woman for knowing how
to make a man's life a burthen to him. Well! I
shall not be here many more days; that's the only
comfort."

His wife looked into his face again, while her lips
began to quiver, and she tried, as she stooped with
the child still in her arms to take something from
the hearth, to take his hand, which hung behind him
as he stood with his back to the fire.

"Bah! Now you'll begin to cry! Well, well!
when a man has put a blister on him, I suppose he
must bear it till it falls off. This is a very pleasant
and cheerful house, Signora Giuditta," he continued,
addressing his guest, who then came down the stairs
with the other child and the cradle, "a *very* plea-

sant house, as I dare say you know, to ask anybody
to come to. Sit down! Here's something to eat,
any way."

The supper was in truth not a very merry one;
and the master of the house felt himself as much
aggrieved as masters of houses under similar circumstances usually do. The women looked at each
other, scarcely daring to utter a word. Giuditta,
when directly appealed to, gave it as her decided
opinion, and as the result of all experience on the
subject, that sending a child to a foundling hospital was the best possible way of securing every
kind of advantage, moral or physical, for it, and
professed her perfect readiness to carry little Stella
to Florence, and her entire satisfaction at the prospect of making the journey under the escort of Il
Gufone. She ate her supper supported by the reflection that it would be the means of saving for
the morrow a plate of beans and oil, which had been
prepared for her evening meal at home, and was
devoutly thankful as soon as she felt herself able
to take her leave of her terrible host, and trot
down the hill, determining, as she went, never
again on any account to let babies, or any question pertaining to them, form any portion of her

frequent gossipings with the idle population of Talamone.

The two women had been effectually prevented from exchanging a syllable save in the presence of the master of the house.   But it was understood to be finally arranged that, on the first day after the return of Signor Nanni Scocco, Signora Giuditta and he should start in charge of little Stella with the *procaccia* who performed the journey between Orbetello and Grosseto, the principal town of the Maremma, should rest there for the night, resume their journey under the care of another *procaccia*, who journeyed between Grosseto and Sienna, and should thence, after another night's rest, travel by diligence to the capital.

CHAPTER VII.

STELLA STARTS ON HER FIRST JOURNEY.

On the evening of the second day after Signora
Giuditta's pleasant supper party, Il Gufone returned home, and was received with somewhat
more kindness than on the occasion of his last
coming. He had, as he reported, been entirely suc-
cessful in his perquisitions.

The Contessa Elena Terrarossa was a widow, who
had become such at a very early age. She had had
no child by her husband the Conte Terrarossa, and
was by no means rich; was, on the contrary, very
poor, the all but entirety of the small property of
her late husband having gone at his death to a
nephew. She was considered, the Gufone said, to
be a very beautiful woman; and it was said that she
might have married more than one rich husband

since her first husband's death. But she had refused all offers, and the report was, that she had loved the younger brother of the Marchese Adriano Casaloni before her marriage with the Conte Terrarossa, and for his sake remained single, though the ecclesiastical career to which he was destined made their attachment a guilty and, in any proper sense, a hopeless one. She was now living in great seclusion and obscurity in Rome; and whether Monsignore Casaloni still visited her or not, Il Gufone confessed that he had not been able to learn with any satisfactory degree of certainty. One thing, however, he had ascertained, he thought, beyond all doubt, having learned it from an old woman who sold hot chestnuts at the corner of a street near that in which the Contessa Elena lived, and who was the mother of a young man who kept company with her maid, and this was, that it had been sorely against her own wishes that her child had been sent away from her, and that that step had been taken entirely in accordance with the will of Monsignore Casaloni, who was terribly afraid of any scandal that might interfere with his own progress towards the highest dignities of the church.

All this Vallardi heard attentively, but without

making any remark on any portion of the information. Then he told his faithful follower that he was to be prepared to accompany the Signora Giuditta and little Stella to Florence on the morrow.

"Stella!" cried Il Gufone, "why, I should have thought—— "

"Yes! you would have thought! Why, where are the brains you boast so much about, you shock-headed owl! Don't you see that I shall have a very pretty card in my hand, to be played some day, when they are least thinking of it, by keeping hold of this countess's bastard! They fancy that I know no more than the Pope who sent the child to me, or who or what she is; and make sure that they will never hear of her again. Ah! they got hold of the wrong man when they pitched on Sandro Vallardi. They should have some such dunderhead as you to deal with, Gufone *mio!* But I suppose you have a sort of glimmering now why Stella must go to the Innocenti, and Leonora must remain here, eh man?"

Il Gufone nodded his great head half-a-dozen times very sententiously, but said nothing.

"And perhaps, too, you may understand another thing;—that it is absolutely necessary that no soul should know that it is not the Roman child that has gone away. Do you hear me? Giuditta Fermi had seen the other brat, and knew it, so I was obliged to tell her; but I don't think she'll say anything," said he with a meaning smile; "she is a very discreet woman, is Giuditta Fermi, when properly handled. As for you, Gufone, we are old friends, and you know me. I mean that nobody shall have a notion of this change between the two children, *e basta!*"

"All right, Signor Sandro. It is no business of mine, you know," returned Il Gufone.

"Just so; no business of yours at all,—except so far as to make it necessary for you to hold your tongue to save your neck from being wrung! That's all!" returned Vallardi with an affectation of carelessness.

"Yes! I know about the kicks; but I am not so clear about the halfpence," snarled Gufone.

"What! aren't you full of supper now, you dog? or do you want more meat and drink? And now mark another thing. See that you behave like a decent human being, as far as you can, and not like an imp of hell, on the journey to Florence and back. You are to play no tricks on this woman, nor tor-

ment her in any way, do you hear! And talking
of tricks, take that, for what you did before starting
for Rome, you cheat-the-hangman hound!" concluded Sandro, hurling a log of wood, which he
had taken from the floor, as though to put it on the
fire, right at Gufone's head. But Nanni was too
practised a player at that game to be worsted at it ;
and a sudden twist of his little body allowed the
wood to fall as harmlessly at the opposite side of
the room, as the plate had done on the former
occasion.

The next morning, Il Gufone and the Signora
Giuditta—the former made as decent as circumstances would allow, with an old jacket and old
hat of his patron's, and carrying the colossal um-
brella and bundle that constituted the Signora
Giuditta's travelling equipage, while that lady herself, who had come up that morning from her own
residence for the purpose, carried the baby—started
on their walk to Orbetello to join the *procaccia*. The
task to be accomplished at Florence was a very
simple one. All that was necessary, was that the
infant should be carried to the Innocenti Hospital
in the Piazza of the Santissima Annunziata in that
city,—that a bell which hangs by the side of a sort

of little hatch-like half-door in the wall of the
building should be pulled, and the child handed
in, when the said hatchway should be opened.
There were no questions to be asked or answered.
But the authorities of the Innocenti do not make a
point of cutting off all means of future communication between the child they receive and those
who send it there, as is the case in some other insti-
tutions founded with a somewhat similar object.
On the contrary, any such means as the persons
leaving a child may choose to supply, are carefully
preserved and registered, so as to be available at
any future period for the recognition of the little
foundling.

It did not appear to have made any part of
Signor Sandro Vallardi's intentions to provide any
such means for the future recognition of his child.
Nor did his wife dare to suggest that any measure
of the kind should be adopted. But at the last
moment, while la Giuditta was laying in a supply
of food, intended to suffice her till she should reach
Grosseto, and Vallardi was giving her during the
process some parting directions, Il Gufone, having
gone into the wood-house at the back of the house
to cut himself a stick, heard himself gently called

by a voice he knew very well, from a window above him.

He looked up without speaking, and at the same instant a bit of blue ribbon came fluttering down by the side of him, with a scrap of paper pinned to it. He took it up, and read, " Give this in with the child." Then he saw too that on the riband there was the word " Stella " worked in red letters. He looked up and nodded his great red head once; then put the paper on the earth, and dug it in with his heel; placed the ribbon carefully in the breast-pocket of his jacket; and ran off to join his travelling companion and begin his journey.

BOOK II.

IN THE MAREMMA.

CHAPTER I.

VERY HARD LINES FOR IL GUFONE.

STELLA VALLARDI was safely deposited in due course at the Innocenti by her two strangely-assorted conductors; and Il Gufone did not forget to execute the commission with which Lucia had entrusted him in the matter related at the close of the last book.

Nanni Scocco, Il Gufone, never did neglect to do any small matters with which the Signora Lucia might occasionally entrust him. He was not in the habit of disregarding the behests of his patron, being admonished thereto, as Signor Sandro had said, by a reasonable regard for his own neck. But it was far more sure that anything which the Signora Lucia might ask of him would be punctually performed.

For Lucia, in her quiet, melancholy, sad way, had
been kind to the strange ungainly boy; and the
extraordinary singularity of such behaviour had
made a remarkable and lasting impression upon
him.

Poor little Giuditta Fermi was the person who
seemed to have suffered most change from the
journey to Florence. She had become singularly
taciturn and uncommunicative. Her gossips
thought that she must be either ill or growing
rich, so little inclination did she show for the
enjoyment of the society she used to be so fond
of. The fact was that the poor woman never in-
dulged herself in a chat without suffering from a
terrible dread that she might allow the secret with
which she was laden to escape her : by dint of
ceaseless vigilance and self-control, however, she
avoided committing the offence which was to bring
down so terrible a penalty upon her. And the fact
that the child which lived and was growing up in
Sandro Vallardi's house was not his own, remained
known only to the four persons who had originally
been cognizant of it.

The little Leonora, at any rate, did not seem to
be affected by the bad nursing with which the

Signora Lucia's husband charged her. The child grew and throve apace. And after a very few days, during which the smart at her heart had made Signora Lucia imagine to herself that she hated the child,—the " brown thing," as she called it,— she not only ceased to hate it, if she had in reality ever done so, but her gentle heart and soft motherly instincts made it become gradually very dear to her.

She was not altogether a child whom a less tender foster-mother would have loved; for she was troublesome, high-spirited, and chancy-tempered. Physically, however, though she was for a while the " brown thing" that Lucia in her first anguish at the loss of her own fair and pink-complexioned darling had called her, she was all that could delight a parent's heart. She seemed to grow perceptibly in loveliness every day, as the weeks rolled themselves into months, the months into years, and the years rolled on. She had an unusually large quantity of the most lovely black silky hair, which made admirable contrast with the dead-white skin of her no longer brown neck and brow. Her great deep liquid eyes seemed to occupy half the surface of the childish little face,

and were shaded with very long black silken lashes,
which lay, when she slept, on the delicate white
cheek below like a deep fringe. The strongly-
arched eyebrow above was already marked in a
delicate dark line on the marble-white forehead.
At seven she was as beautiful a little fairy as can be
imagined. At twelve she was lanky, long-looking
in face, and body, and limbs; almost gaunt in the
leanness of her face and figure, the thin fleshless-
ness of her dark yet *mate* white cheeks, and the
portentous largeness of the great, wide-opened,
earnest-looking eyes. Yet to those who were competent judges of the symptoms and foreshadowings
in such matters, it was even then evident that the
lapse of some three or four more years would find
the little Leonora Vallardi—for such she was supposed to be by all the world around her—a very
lovely girl.

So much for her progress towards physical perfection. The facts of the case are told in a few
words, and are very easily imagined and understood;
but the history of the moral and intellectual training which, consciously or unconsciously, intention-
ally or unintentionally administered, to good result
or to evil result, she was picking up during the

same time, cannot be quite so easily told, or so readily comprehended.

Of all the agencies around her which contributed, or might be supposed to have contributed, to that fashioning of her mind and heart which is usually designated by the vaguely general term education, her supposed father, Sandro Vallardi, was the one who had the smallest influence. Sandro was year by year less and less at home. His absences were longer than ever, and succeeded each other mostly with but a few days, or at most a week or two, of interval. By degrees, too, his wife, as well as everybody else who was in any degree honoured by his acquaintance in and about Talamone, began unconsciously at first to feel that the periods of his absence were better times than the shorter intervals of his presence at home. Life in the lone house in the woods upon the hill above Talamone went on tolerably enough when the master of it was away. If it could hardly be said that there was any great amount of happiness there,—especially as concerned the lone woman who carried so many an imperfectly cicatrised sorrow in her heart, —there was at least a certain degree of quiet content. The tears were less often in the Signora

Lucia's eyes than used to be the case. As for
the little Leonora,—it is generally supposed and
accepted that children are always happy, simply by
virtue of their childhood. The theory is perhaps
less accurately correct than pleasant. But the fact
is that it is often very difficult to tell whether a
child is happy or not. Of course some may be
seen to be very evidently happy; and more, alas!
may be, with very little danger of error, pronounced
to be very decidedly the reverse. But how many
little, silent, undemonstrative hearts there are, of
which who shall say what the shy reticence and
proud want of confidence covers! Pride, I take it,
enters far more largely into the causes of childhood's communications or non-communications with
the world around it than is generally imagined.

What amount of aught that can be called happiness fell to the lot of little Leonora during those
years of her life at Talamone it would be hard to
say. She was by no means a communicative child;
though, save on rare occasions, not ungentle, and
within the very small circle of those on whom it
was possible for her to bestow love, by no means
unloving. Lucia had long since come to love her
as if she had been indeed her own; and Leonora, it

could not be doubted, loved her dearly in return.
Next to Lucia, what human being was there near
her on whom affection could be expended? Il
Gufone was the only other member of the little
household as it was constituted during the times of
Sandro's absence, which covered at least nine-tenths
of the year. Gufone was now mostly at home.
From time to time Sandro would take him away
with him; and no word ever fell from Nanni
Scocco's lips when he returned to Talamone to throw
any light on the cause, the nature, or the where-
abouts of these excursions. But, for the most part,
Sandro took the habit of leaving him at home
during these years. The "family" in the lone
house on the promontory then generally consisted
of a trio,—the Signora Lucia, little Leonora, and
Nanni Scocco, Il Gufone.

It may seem to most readers,—more especially to
any of the gentler sex and of still blooming cheeks,
whose eyes these pages may be fortunate enough to
meet,—that Il Gufone, as the reader knows him,
was not a promising object for the investment of
any of the treasures of affection which the young
heart is always seeking some opportunity of "putting out" to advantage. Nevertheless it was the

fact that Leonora loved Il Gufone as well, if not
better, than she loved Lucia. It is not of course
the love of a maiden that I am speaking of, but
that of a child.   And though Leonora, if Nanni
Scocco had been for the first time presented to her,
—say at ten or twelve years old,—would probably
have run from him with terror and repugnance;
yet, having known his great shock red head, and
ugly white face, and grotesque shuffling limbs, as
one of the phenomena of the outward world with
which she had earliest become acquainted, and
having, on the other hand, invariably found that
this gnome was not a baneful creature, but for her
at least a beneficent one, Leonora, in the utter
absence of any more promising investment, had
invested a large amount of surplus love capital in
the Gufone.

Among other matters in which the gnome had
been found beneficent, he had been the main agent
in the child's education, in the more restricted
sense of the term. The Signora Lucia when a girl
would have been returned in the census, if Italy
had in those days dreamed of such statistical
luxuries, as among the number of those who could
read and write; and at her marriage she had signed

her own name in the register.   But if poor Lucia at
the time now spoken of had been required to give
any proof of her acquirements in either reading or
writing, she would probably have shown that if
reading and writing " come by nature," they may
also quite completely go by an entirely natural
process.

Now Nanni Scocco, the Gufone, could not only
read and write, but could do both these things
readily and well.   It was strange, perhaps, that
such should be the case.   But in Roman Catholic
communities, ruled as Italy was ruled in those days,
the dispensation of the elements of education among
the people is not so much absolutely null as capri-
cious.   Of course the clergy are the only educators.
Of course any large scheme for the educating of
the nation would have been an abomination and
an utterly intolerable absurdity to their minds.
But the Roman Catholic clergy have never been
averse from educating, after their own fashion, such
odds and ends of humanity as happened to come
immediately under their hands, and were not too
numerous to be dealt with by irregular and individual exertion.   Specially they have been willing
to give such instruction as they know how to give,

to any of the various classes of individuals who are
hangers-on in any way of their own order, aco-
lytes, chorister boys, sacristans, cross-bearers, and
such like.

Now the probability is that Nanni Scocco had
picked up his education, or rather the means of
educating himself, in some such capacity. It would
have been a tolerably safe bet that Il Gufone had
at one time of his life been familiar with the in-
terior of a sacristy; and it would be quite in
accordance with the experience that any one may
gather from a fairly wide field of observation in
the ecclesiastical strata of Roman Catholic society,
if it were supposed that the moral education which
adapted him for the purposes to which Sandro
Vallardi put him, and which cropped out in such
manifestations of idiosyncrasy as have been recorded
of Il Gufone, was gathered from the same field
which had furnished the intellectual training of
which we have been speaking.

The fact is that poor Nanni Scocco had been
furnished by nature, as he so often boasted, with
a larger allowance of brains than she often allots
to more daintily and preciously-fashioned brain-
caskets. Had other matters been " in a concatena-

tion accordingly," Nanni would doubtless have been
called and recognised as a very clever fellow. As
it was, the world considered that nothing better
than a half-wit could dwell within such a head;
and behaving to him always in accordance with
this theory, had produced in him a strangely dis-
torted and twisted mental fabric, curiously mottled
with information and ignorance, shrewdness and
imbecility, cross-grained perverseness and loving
tenderness, respect for knowledge and hostility
towards the classes of society mainly in possession
of it. And this curiously gnarled spirit, inhabiting
the strangely repulsive frame the reader wots of,
had been the principal guide, philosopher, and
friend of the child who was now rapidly growing
into a rarely lovely woman;—her master, pastor,
and spiritual teacher; the companion of her wanderings about the shores, and woods, and crags; her
protector, when she ventured into the haunts of
men and the great world, as represented by the
town and port of Talamone; and the source of all
the knowledge she possessed beyond such as the
opening of her eyes on the world around her could
impart.

And, as I have said, the child loved her strange

companion with a strong child's love; loved him
as one may see a strong-hearted child love a dog
or other such companion! Any intimation that the
ungainly creature could claim the rank of a fellow-
creature,—that he was in any sense of the same
nature or order of being as herself,—would probably have revolted Leonora terribly.   Of course
no definite thought of the kind, or indeed upon the
subject at all, had ever crossed her mind, but it
was her none the less real because unrecognised
feeling.

As for the poor Gufone himself, his feeling
towards his pupil was the only form of worship
that his mind had ever known;—and doubtless
he was, poor ungraced creature! infinitely the
better for even that form of it.

The only other person whom the child Leonora
saw sufficiently often to learn to know her was
Giuditta Fermi.   She never by any chance came
near the lone house on the promontory on the
rare occasions when the master of it was at home.
She would always, indeed, contrive, if possible, at
such times to go away, the further the better, from
Talamone and its neighbourhood, to the house of
some one of her country clients.   It was somehow

or other always very well known at Talamone
when Signor Sandro Vallardi was at home. And
when she was sure that he was away, Giuditta
would very often stroll up the hill in the evening,
to look in on Signora Lucia, and have a bit of
supper and chat. There was never any great
straightness of means in Signor Vallardi's house.
His unkindness to his wife never took the form of
stinting her in the necessities of life, and the very
modest comforts to which she had been accustomed.
Very little money was needed for the supply of all
that the little family required, and money always
came in abundantly sufficient amounts for all those
small requirements. The appearance of the Signora
Giuditta a little before the supper-hour was always
very welcome to Lucia. It was the only point of
contact with the world of her fellow-creatures that
existed for her; and for poor Giuditta, Lucia was
the only person with whom she could talk with
freedom from the never-absent dread that she should
drop some dreadful word which might be the means
of bringing down upon her head that terrible sword
of vengeance that she knew was always suspended
above it.

Il Gufone could not be said to be the only

instructor of Leonora. Lucia, though her teachings
did not take the semblance of "book learning,"
also taught the child much ; and her teachings were
not the less valuable that they were of a nature
which the child's character especially needed, and
which she was for that reason the less disposed
easily to assimilate and profit by. The things that
Lucia had learned in a school which impresses its
lessons more deeply than her teachers of the art of
reading and writing had done in her case, and
which she therefore was well qualified to teach in
her turn, were resignation, gentleness of heart and
of temper, long-suffering without loud complaint,
and an imperishable faith in the conviction that
loving is better than hating,—that a woman's happiness in the world is to be loved, and her part and
her duty to love.

Thus Lucia and Il Gufone had both their parts
in Leonora's training ; but I do not think that
the third of the trio which formed her world—La
Giuditta—did much in the same direction. It may
be feared, indeed, that her frequent presence did
somewhat to counteract some of Lucia's teaching ;
for by the time she was twelve years old, poor
Giuditta became the butt against which many of the

sharp arrows of Leonora's ridicule and caustic wit
were directed. Nor did her other instructor at all
counteract this tendency; on the contrary, he was
the partner and the accomplice in many a prank
played off at poor Giuditta's expense, and many a
quip and sally of which she was the frequently
unconscious victim.

And thus the years went on, till all of a sudden,
as it seemed to the Gufone, Leonora began to show
that she did not like to be carried across the
mountain streams, which often had to be crossed in
their pathless wanderings, in the arms of her companion. Nanni combated this at first, assuring her
that there was no danger, that he was strong enough
to carry her though she were twice as heavy, and
upbraiding her with having turned coward all at
once. Then one day a sudden conception, a flash
of enlightenment, darted through his mind like an
electric shock! His white face suddenly became a
deeper red than his fiery hair. He turned away
with his head bent downwards towards the earth, as
though he had been lashed; and he never proposed
to carry Leonora again.

Little rest had the poor Gufone that night, toss-
ing and tumbling about in feverish attempts to

make it clear to himself whether he most loved
or most hated the beautiful child, who had thus
silently and treacherously grown into a beautiful
maiden, and made him wretched.   He told himself that he hated her, and always would hate
her, and should feel a pleasure in clutching her
slender throat with his bony long fingers, till he
had squeezed the life out of her.   And then he
writhed in his truckle bed, and turned his face to
the wall and burst into bitter tears,—the first
bitter tears that he could ever remember to have
shed.   And much he marvelled at himself, and
thought that he must be ill in body.   Was it the
fever that had clutched him, too, at last?   He
knew only that he was very miserable, and that
somehow it was Leonora's fault.   And then he fell
to devising schemes for making it manifest to her
how bitterly he hated her.

And so, being utterly unable to sleep, he rose
and stole silently from the house, and laboured
during the midnight hours at hewing in the wood,
and raising in their places the upright posts, to
form the framework of a summer-house, which
Leonora had the day before set her heart upon
building on a crag of the promontory which com-

manded a lovely view of the sea, and the Monte Argentario in the distance.   Poor Gufone!

Then, when at last the morning came, it was worse.   For Leonora would not understand that the night work bestowed upon the summer-house meant anything else, except that good old Gufo was anxious to please her as he always was.   And she thanked him as gaily and unconstrainedly as if he had really done it because he meant to please her, and took no heed whatever of the sombre looks which were meant to express to her how far otherwise the real state of the case was, and did not seem the least bit in the world sorry that he should have thus laboured for her.   To Leonora it would indeed have seemed strange if Gufo had not been only too happy to spend his night, or his day either, in doing her will.

For all this, the readings, and the writing, and the explanations of difficulties did not cease, though Gufone swore to himself every night that they should do so the next day.   But the next day came, and was passed as the day before it and its predecessors had been passed.   And Leonora grew more beautiful every day, and became, as Nanni continually told his only confidant,

—himself,—prouder and prouder the prettier she grew!

She was between fifteen and sixteen when the period of life to which these notices belong had been reached.   And it was only a few months after that time that events came to pass which effectually changed both the tenour of her life and the current of her thoughts.

CHAPTER II.

CESARE CASALONI.

ABOUT that time, when, as I have stated, events happened which powerfully influenced the future life and fortunes of Leonora Casaloni,—or Leonora Vallardi, as she was known to the world of Talamone,—some larger events happened, which were also powerfully influential on a larger scale. It was the time of one of those many upheavings of the volcanic social soil of Italy which preceded the great, and, let us hope, final eruption of 1859. There were many of these premature attempts to throw off the incubus which pressed with intolerable weight on the vitals of the country,—attempts which ended only in the ruin and wretchedness of many families, in executions, exile, and confiscation, and which Europe, witnessing with pain these, as

it seemed, inevitable results, stigmatised as unwise
and deplorable, however heroic,—whereby Europe
showed its own lack of faith in sundry eternal
truths. The heroic self-sacrifice operated according
to its nature, however, to the results ordained to
follow from such efforts, despite the want of faith
in the spectators of the drama, and produced its
fruit in due season. And those who are discontented with the fruit that has been produced, may
be consoled with the assurance that there is better
fruit to come,—none of which could have been
matured without the sacrifices which prepared the
possibilities of it.

It was mainly and most frequently in the States
of the Church that these outbreaks used to occur.
But government was there at its worst; and the
mingled temporal and spiritual tyranny and oppression made it more galling and utterly intolerable than the burthen of lay tyrannies, however
heavy. The March of Ancona and Romagna was
the principal scene of the outbreak which occurred
at the time here alluded to. That long, narrow
strip of exceedingly fertile alluvial soil which lies
between the Apennine and the Adriatic, crowded
with populous cities, which grew into celebrity in

the arts, in literature, and in commerce under the
stormy rule of their independent mediæval princes,
only to sink into effeteness and decay under the
leaden uniformity of priestly despotism, is inhabited
by a race which has always shown itself impatient
of tyranny. Again and again they rose against
the terrified despots, whose repeated successes in
crushing such outbreaks did not avail to temper the
cruelties prompted by terror with any of the moderation of conscious strength. And again and again
these attempts, born of desperation, were quelled
and quenched in the blood of the best and worthiest
of the population. Always the old Tarquinian
teaching was observed. The tallest and finest
flowers were selected for the cutting down. Any
baseness of tergiversation or treachery found ready
mercy in the tenderness of a Church which does
not desire the death of any sinner,—except those
whom it fears.

In the insurrection of which mention has here
been made, many young men belonging to the
upper classes took part, and some bearing the
names of the great families of the Roman aris-
tocracy. It is hardly necessary to say that all
these were very young men. Age is more apt to

bear the ills it has, instead of flying to those it knows of but too well. And the experiences of any life-time of ordinary duration were sufficient in those socially volcanic regions to show what were the immediate results to be expected from such tentatives.

I have spoken of the heroism displayed in these hapless attempts; without much of which they would never have taken place. But it does not follow that all who were concerned in them were heroes. Generous impulses, in a certain measure, assuredly animated by far the greater number of them. Some were doubtless induced to join in efforts to overturn the established order of things by motives of the nature of those ascribed by Sallust to the followers of Catiline. A smaller number made the opportunities afforded by such effort serve as a screen for mere brigandage. And perhaps a very few professed to join in the revolutionary schemes with the intention from the first of making profit by betraying them.

But those who willingly risked their lives and possessions in the hope of ameliorating the social condition of their country were not all heroes,—as those who know somewhat of human nature and of revolutionary movements will readily understand,— not all heroes any more than all those who can feel poetry, and would fain produce it, are all poets. They had heroic tendencies; but then the tares spring up,—the flesh, the world, and the devil never fail to sow them thick enough in the fields planted with youthful heroisms; and many heroes of twenty are at thirty disposed to limit their aspirations to Respectability, let the powers that be, on the side of which that rate-and-tax-paying divinity always ranges herself, be what they may.

Among those compromised by the outbreak in question was a young man of the Casaloni family, and, from the circumstances of the family, a very important member of it. The Marchese Adriano, the head of the family, had been disappointed in early life both in love and in such ambition as it is possible for a lay grandee of the Apostolic Roman court to conceive. The result had been, that while still a comparatively young man, he had retired to the huge and gloomy villa on his ancestral property in the neighbourhood of Mon-tamiata,—a very remarkable, richly-wooded moun-tain, situated close to the southern confines between Tuscany and the Roman States, and had lived

there ever since unmarried and in great retirement.
At the time in question he was a man of some
fifty years, being at least ten years the senior of
his brother Ercole, who was pushing his fortunes in
the ecclesiastical career, with good hope of receiving
in due time the earthly crown due to his merits,
in the shape of a scarlet hat.

The career, however, which had thus been selected
for the younger brother of the great house precluded
the idea of any continuation of the family tree pro-
ceeding from him. The family honours might,
and no doubt would be, duly and largely increased
by his contributions to them; but the heirs to these
and all the rest of the family greatness must be
provided from some other source. There was no
third brother living, and it had become evident now
to the Marchese himself, if not to others, that no
legitimate heir to the Casaloni name and estates
would ever be born to him. Under these circumstances he had, three or four years before the time
in question, called to him a cousin of the house, a
certain Cesare Casaloni, then a lad of some four-
teen or fifteen years old. He, it was determined,
should be the heir of all the family greatness, and
the transmitter of it to future generations. Of

course the lad's parents, far-off cousins of the great
family, desired nothing better, nor did, at least in
the first instance, the lad himself.   He and his
parents lived in Rome, and he had been intended
for the Church ; but having violently and successfully struggled against that destiny, and being a
remarkably tall and handsome youth, it had been
hoped by his family that, by the assistance of his
cousin, the Monsignore, a commission might be
obtained for him in the noble corps of the Papal
Guards.   And in the hope of that superficially and
personally splendid, but, in reality, very meagre
promotion, he was waiting till his moustaches
should be grown, and Fortune be ready to lend
him a helping hand, when the family Jupiter, the
Marchese Adriano, came to the determination above
stated.

The young Cesare was to go at once to the Villa
Casaloni, at the foot of Montamiata, there to live
under the guidance of a tutor, and in the worshipful
company of the Marchese, such a life as should be
a fitting preparation for the high destiny which
awaited him.   The boy went, nothing loth.   What
sort of thing life in a splendid villa at the foot of
Montamiata might be, he was naturally able to

imagine to himself but very imperfectly. He knew
that he should have a gun of his own, and he ascertained that there was much game in the Montamiata
woods. Probably, had he been a year older, he
might have interested himself in inquiring what
sort of human surroundings he might expect to
find in his new abode. But interest in, and information respecting such particulars, came together
at a somewhat later date.

Cesare came to Villa Casaloni, and found himself
the victim of a series of disillusions and disappoint-
ments. It was not that the villa was less magnificent than he had imagined it,—but it was very
dull! It was not that his cousin the Marchese was
less kind to him than he had hoped,—but the
Marchese was portentously dull! It was not that
the priest assigned him as a tutor was more severe
or less respectful than he had expected,—but the
Rev. Michele Profondi was awfully dull! The
whole life around him and before him was of a
leaden dulness of which the boy, accustomed to the
life of Rome, had never formed a conception. And
dulness is one of the few human evils which becomes
not more tolerable, but more intolerable, by the
duration of it.

The Marchese had but one subject of thought, of study, or of conversation,—the family greatness, the family honours, the family genealogy; and though the young man, who had been suddenly called to the ownership and enjoyment of all these things, was at first not unwilling to listen to the detailed account of all the magnificence that was to be his, he soon became dreadfully bored by the constant repetition of it.

Then, although his family at Rome had always been among those who were known to be entirely well-affected to the Papal Government, the lad himself had frequented company which, had they been aware of the fact, would have been highly dis-approved by his seniors, and which had, to a certain degree, inoculated him with liberalising notions and tendencies. He was not without some tincture of tastes and studies, the nature of which inclined his mind in that direction. The gods had made him poetical! He had read Dante, and Alfieri, and Filicaja; and had himself indited sonnets on the stock subject of Italy's past glories and present decadence. There was not the stuff in him which could have prevented him from very genuinely pre-ferring to be a wealthy marchese to being a poverty-

stricken poet or patriot, but there was enough of
the froth of liberalistic and revolutionary notions
and sentiments fermenting in his mind, to render
him discontented with a system of things which
made itself specially manifest to him in the shape
of a life too dreadfully dreary to be tolerated.

It had thus come to pass that, when the conspirators who had organised the movement that has
been alluded to, thought that the time was ripe for
insurrection, young Cesare Casaloni, then eighteen
years old, had joined them ;—of course to the
infinite horror, disgust, and indignation of his
relative the Marchese ;—and, indeed, of all his
relatives whatever.   Of course the abortive attempt
was very soon put down, and the time of proscrip-
tions, condemnations, confiscations, executions, and
hunting-down began.   The Government were in
possession of very accurate information as to the
names of all those who had committed themselves
by any outward act, especially of such as belonged
by their connections to the upper ranks of society.
There had been nothing like fighting.   The matter
had not been allowed to go far enough for that.
But it was known, and was undeniable, that Cesare
Casaloni had attended a certain meeting held at

the dwelling of one of the principal leaders of the movement in the city of Rimini;—all that passed at which was known to the Government with the utmost accuracy of detail;—and also that he had been present at a much larger meeting of conspirators, with arms in their hands, at a lonely spot among the lower slopes of the Apennine, not very far from the same city. And no more than this was needed to make him a proscribed man, for the capture of whom the officers of the Government were very anxious.

It was towards the latter end of October that young Cesare Casaloni found himself very hard-pressed by the bloodhounds of the *sbirri*, who were bent on capturing him. He had escaped, with difficulty, from Rimini, together with one companion, in a small fishing-boat, which had landed them as night was setting in on a lonely part of the coast a little to the southward of that city. Their hope in embarking had been no more than this. The fisherman, who was with difficulty persuaded to render the two young men this service, had no idea of remaining out all night, nor had they any sort of provision for a longer voyage. Nevertheless, the good office rendered them by the

boat was a very important one. They were out of
Rimini; and it would have been very difficult for
them to have accomplished even thus much in any
other way.

Having been safely landed on the beach in the
immediate neighbourhood of the mouth of the river
Marrano, in the first dusk of the rapidly-fading
twilight, it became necessary, in the first place, to
determine on their further course. And in the
short and hurried debate which arose upon this
question, the two fugitives differed in opinion.
Casaloni's companion, a young Neapolitan, wished
to keep near to the coast, and make southwards.
The great post-road from Bologna to Ancona,
passing through Rimini and the other cities which
thickly stud the lowlands between the Apennine
and the Adriatic, runs at no great distance from
the coast in this part of its course. And Casaloni
urged the danger of the immediate neighbourhood
of such a great highway, as a reason for preferring
to strike into the mountains. Moreover, another
motive was active in the case of his companion,
which did not influence him. The young Neapolitan was anxious to return to his home. Casaloni
had no home to which he could return. To have

presented himself at the Villa Casaloni under his present circumstances would, he felt, have been almost, if not quite, as bad as walking into a guard-house of the Pope's soldiers. The result was that the two fugitives determined to separate; —a resolution which they came to the more readily from the well-founded belief that ultimate escape would be more possible for a single wanderer than for two compromised individuals travelling together.

The young Neapolitan, therefore, accompanying his comrade only so far inland as was necessary to avoid the danger of passing too close to a post of coastguards established, as their friend the fisherman had cautioned them, at a lone tower called the Torre de Trinita, at the embouchure of the Marrano, then struck off southwards. And Casaloni, not without a somewhat bitter feeling, probably, that the dulness of the Villa Casaloni was yet preferable to that of a lonely night on the flank of the Apennine, pursued his way towards the mountains.

He was not very far distant from the frontier of the little Republic of San Marino; and it is likely enough that the sound of that appellation carried with it a hope of safety to the ears of the young conspirator. But it would have been a grievous blunder to have trusted to any protection to be found in the franchises or the liberalism of the miniature republic. For the republican authorities know too well that their eight-century old independence would have but very small chance of becoming any older if they were to suffer their little territory to be made the asylum of any political proscript, or, indeed, of any fugitive whatsoever, from the grasp of their powerful neighbours. And a stranger from a city reeking with pestilence would not be repulsed from a community trembling for its own safety more rigorously than a proscribed rebel flying from the vengeance of the holy father.

Chance, however, or the nature of the ground, and the direction of the little valleys which lay more intricately among the hills as he neared the higher mountains, saved him from the commission of this error.

Behind the little town of San Marino, which is perched on a lofty cliff, the highest point of its little territory, there is a very lonely and wild part of the Apennine. The town, on its lofty and isolated eminence, faces towards the Adriatic and the opposite coast of Dalmatia, which may be seen from the battlements of its ancient castle. By the phrase "behind the town" is meant, therefore, the region to the westward, extending towards Tuscany. The existence of the Tuscan frontier in this direction afforded also a very well-founded reason for choosing the course which Casaloni had chosen, for when once this should have been crossed he would be comparatively safe. The Grand Ducal Government at that time was on perfectly friendly terms with that of Rome, and would not have replied by a negative to any demand for the extradition of a political fugitive; but the Tuscan Government would have avoided complying with the demand if they could have found any colourable means of doing so. And certainly no Tuscan official would spontaneously give himself any trouble to arrest or interfere with one merely suspected of being such. To reach the Tuscan frontier would therefore be a great point gained. The country between it and the labyrinth of intricate valleys into which Casaloni had found his way is a very wild and thinly-inhabited one. The main danger had already been surpassed when the thickly-inhabited low country, and the neighbourhood of its towns, and numerous large rich villages, was left behind him.

Wandering onwards, almost without any object
save that of gradually making westward as far as
he could, and of finding some place at which it
would not be too dangerous to ask for shelter for
the night, he had gradually climbed to a considerable height on the mountain side, chiefly because he
had felt that among the sinuosities of the valleys he
was losing all certainty of the direction in which
he was going. Gradually, too, the country he was
traversing was becoming wilder and more entirely
desolate; and he began to fear that he should be
obliged to lay himself down on the bare hill-side
supperless as he was, and so await what the morning light should bring. But just as he was resign-
ing himself to this course his ear caught the sound
of a not very distant bell. As far as he could see,
he was on the open side of an utterly trackless
mountain waste,—a very unlikely place to find any
village, however poor and small. He made his way,
however, towards the sound without much difficulty,
for the ground was entirely open. There was
neither enclosure, fence, nor any sign of cultivation
on all the bleak hill-side.

Presently he came to the building above which
the bell was ringing,—a very small but strongly-

built edifice, with a strong door deeply recessed in
its round-arched doorway ; a little hermitage, or
" eremo," as it called itself, or small priory belonging to a Franciscan convent situated at a not very
far distant, but less bleak and desolate, part of the
mountain. It frequently occurs that the convents
of the austerer orders, situated in solitary parts of
the mountains, have outposts, as it were, placed in
yet more dreary, exposed, and desolate parts of the
mountain, to which brethren are sent out from the
principal establishment, either as a measure of discipline or as a means and proof of extra sanctity.

It was such an establishment, of a very humble
and modest kind, situated some few miles distant
from a larger Franciscan convent on the same lofty
and desolate hill-top, called the Monte di Carpegno,
that Casaloni had fallen in with. Had it been a
police bureau, with the Papal arms and cross-keys
over the door, the fugitive would almost have been
tempted to enter, so dead beat was he, and so terrible seemed the prospect of wandering about shelter-
less and without food on that hill-side all the night,
But in truth he could hardly have fallen in with a
safer asylum for the night at least. It was not that
the friars might be expected to sympathise at all

with the cause which had made him a proscript
and fugitive, or that it might be safe to trust to
their hospitality for too long a period;—not for so
long a period, perhaps, as might suffice for a slow-
crawling monk, with his *besace* over his shoulder, to
wander down the mountain to Rimini, and for a
brisker police-agent to climb from Rimini to the
little priory. But for some hours the Franciscan
hermitage was as safe a harbour as he could wish,
and he was quite sure of not being refused admit-
tance. These mountain convents and priories deem
it part of their especial duty to give shelter and some
modicum of such food as they have to travellers.

Casaloni pulled the great iron ring at the end of
the large chain that hung by the side of the clamped
and nailed door, and in a minute a ponderous bolt
was heard grating in its staple, and a gaunt, spare,
barefooted figure in brown serge, with knotted cord
around his attenuated body, appeared in answer to
the summons. There was no delay in responding
to it, for the little community, consisting of four
members, as Casaloni soon learned, was afoot, and
the bell which he had heard was ringing for the
service of the first canonical hour of the night.

" I have been out shooting, *frate mio*," said Casaloni, "and have been belated, and lost my way; and was thinking that I must lay me down on the bare ground, when I heard your bell. And if I don't find shelter with you, I must lie here at your gate, for I am too tired to go any farther."

"*Passi, signore,*" said the friar, opening wide the door, and standing aside to let the stranger enter. "Of course such shelter and food as we have is yours for the claiming of it; but it is but little of either we have to offer, and you must share that little with another, for you are not the first comer to the door to-night."

The announcement was rather startling to Casaloni, for it struck him that the belated stranger who had been a little beforehand with him might well be some one of those who were out in search of him and others similarly wanted. Still, another moment of reflection told him that *sbirri* and *giandarmi* rarely move save in pairs; and, at all events, he had by that time passed the doorway, and the friar had closed and rebolted the door with a reverberating bang.

CHAPTER III.

A FRIEND IN NEED IS NOT ALWAYS A FRIEND INDEED.

CESARE CASALONI found himself in a very small flag-paved open court of irregular triangular shape, on which the entrance-door opened beneath a low-browed arch, over which was a portion of the upper story of the building. On one side the little space was enclosed by the west front-door of the small and humble chapel, over which was a slightly-elevated peak of wall, in an open triangular-shaped hole in which hung the bell which had attracted his steps to the building. Over the doorway, which together with a dark wood-house on one side, and an equally dark sort of cellar and general store-room on the other, occupied all that side of the court, was a couple of rooms, evidently the best in the building;

and these were the guest chambers, appropriated
for the reception of travellers who sought the hospitality of the hermitage. The third side of the court,
which looked as if it had grown into its queer
irregularity of form rather than been built so in
accordance with any plan, was occupied by the little
refectory and smaller kitchen on the ground floor,
and half-a-dozen little bits of cells on the story
above. And this constituted the entirety of the
small priory.

The entire community, with the exception of the
porter, who was also bell-ringer, sacristan, cook, and
attendant on strangers,—all the rest of the community, numbering three souls, were *in coro*,—in
the little chapel, performing the first choral service
of the night. The stranger within their gates was
not apparently availing himself of the privilege of
joining in their devotions, for there was a light
visible in the shutterless windows of the room over
the gateway. Casaloni's guide turned to a very
small round arched doorway under the archway of
entrance, so placed as to be at right angles to the
outer door, and opening it, showed a narrow and
very steep stone stair, which led to the rooms above.
The young man followed him, not without some

anxiety as to what manner of man his fellow-guest might prove to be. He is, at all events, thought Casaloni, not so tired as I am, or he would already be in bed and asleep.

His conductor opened another small door at the head of the stair, and Casaloni found himself in the presence of the man whose supper and chamber he was to share. The outer room, or that first reached from the stair, was a little sitting or eating room; and the second room opening from it a sleeping-chamber, provided with a couple of beds.

It was very bare—the little sitting-room—but perfectly clean; for the mendicants do not seem to think it necessary to apply the same rule of mortification by dirt to their habitations which they carry out so rigorously in their own persons. The boarded floor of the little room was quite clean, the white deal table in the middle of it was clean, and the rush-bottomed purgatorially-constructed chairs were clean. There was a fireplace very large for the size of the room, and a large fire was blazing in it; for though it was only October, and the weather was still fine, and even hot down on the lowlands by the coast, a good fire was by no means an unnecessary luxury on the bleak top of the Monte Carpegno.

And the previous occupant of the room was enjoying this portion of the friars' hospitality to the utmost. There were but four small rush-bottomed chairs in the room; and of these he was occupying three, placed so as to serve as nearly as was possible the purpose of a sofa in front of the blazing beech-logs. Close to his elbow, on the narrow stone mantel-shelf, was an emptied flask of red wine.

The stranger was a tall and strikingly handsome man, whose black hair and abundant black beard were beginning to be very sparsely streaked with threads of silver. His long and well-shaped limbs, clothed in brown cloth breeches and leathern gaiters, were thrown with a not inelegant careless-ness over the chairs he was monopolising; and his handsome head was thrown back, so as to lean against the corner formed by the projection of the fireplace. He did not rise, or in any way change his lounging position, when Casaloni entered; but he raised from his head the soft black felt hat, which was overshadowing his brows, in somewhat careless salutation, and then replaced it without speaking.

"Good evening, signore!" said Casaloni. "I

am afraid that it is hardly a case of 'the more the merrier' in these quarters; and that you would have fared all the better if I had not been belated on the mountain, as I suppose you were also."

"Umph!" said the stranger with a shrug; "there are a couple of beds in that kennel in there, and I never use more than one at a time, and am not particular as to my chamber-mates. But I was not belated on the mountain myself, any more than you were!"

The friar had by this time left the room to get the new-comer something to eat, and the two strangers were alone. Casaloni stared at the man who uttered the above somewhat rude speech a little uneasily before he replied.

"As for me," he said, "I certainly was belated, as you may see for yourself; and I am sure I can't guess what on earth else should bring a man to such a place as this at this time of night."

"Well, I don't know," said the stranger carelessly, without moving from his lounging attitude. "I should have thought that many a motive might bring a man here; as, for instance, the necessity of escaping from the Holy Father's *sbirri*, after conspiring against his Government."

Casaloni changed colour, and started visibly; but in the next instant, assuming an air of careless ease, he drew the fourth chair to the other corner of the fireplace, and sat down over the fire.

"I suppose," he said, after reflection for a minute or two, "that you know me; though I have not a notion where I have ever seen you before. But I imagine you are not inclined to do the work of the Pope's spies for them."

"I!" said the stranger; "bless your soul, no! Not I! When I want a score of scudi or so, which occurs now and then, I know of an honester way of coming by them than by turning a priest's spy for them. No; you are in no danger from me."

"So I should have supposed. Perhaps you were one of us in this last affair."

"Look here," said the stranger, touching his beard with his finger.

"What do you mean?" said Casaloni. "If that is one of the signs, it is one that they have not taught me, and——"

"It is a sign that may be understood without any teaching," said the other. "Don't you see the white hairs in my beard? I take it all the beards of your friends who were concerned in this affair were black, or maybe brown, weren't they? No grey ones, I fancy, eh?"

"Ah! I see what you mean now. I suppose we were all, or pretty well all, young men," replied Casaloni, simply.

"All, to a man, you may take your oath. Ah, old fellows have had enough of all that, and have given up the profitable game of kicking against the pricks, before they come to my age, you may swear. But it's no business of mine. I've no objection to the young 'uns having their fling of fun, not I!"

"But where have you known me?" rejoined Casaloni, looking at the stranger's strikingly handsome face more attentively than he had yet done; "I cannot remember to have seen you before. But since you know who I am," he continued, "perhaps you can give me news of the Marchese?"

"Where was he when you left him?" asked the stranger, speaking with apparent carelessness.

"At Villa Casaloni to be sure! I don't think he has left it for a night for years past," replied the young man, suffering himself to be pumped with the utmost facility.

"The old fellow will not have been very well

pleased at your meddling with business of this sort," said Vallardi—for he it was.

The remark was a very safe one ; for Sandro knew quite enough of the Marchese to be very sure that he would not approve of anybody whatever being concerned in an insurrection against the Government. When Casaloni had first entered the room he had not the smallest idea who or what he was ; but he knew of course that a plan of insurrection had been detected and crushed, and that the Papal troops and *giandarmi* and *sbirri* were busily engaged in hunting down those of the compromised who had escaped. And the nature of the place, the geographical locality, and the appearance of the young man, had led him to form a shrewd guess which Casaloni's simplicity had at once converted into a certainty. It still remained for Sandro to discover who the new-comer really was.

" The Marchese," he said, "will not have approved of your being in a business of this kind ! "

"Approve ! No, *per Dio ;* I should think not ! I have ruined myself root and branch there. I should think the old boy would rather that the name of Casaloni should never be heard of

again, than that it should be inherited by a
Liberal, let alone an insurgent!"

"Is there any other of the family whom he
could put into your place?" said Vallardi, who
was well aware that the old Marchese Casaloni
had taken into his house a young and distant
member of the family as his future heir, and who
had now learned pretty well all he wanted to know
with regard to the stranger.

"No, I think not! Not so far as I know;—none
of the name!" said Cesare.

"Well, then, I think that you need not give up,
Signor Marchese. You will come round to the top
of the wheel one of these days. And as for the
Marchese, you will never have to ask him to forgive
you, signore. I had a mind to be sure that I was
not mistaken in you before speaking. But I am
able to tell you that the Marchese died suddenly
the night before last."

"Good God!" exclaimed the young man, with
a sudden change of colour which marked the im-
pressionable nervousness of his temperament; "are
you sure of what you are saying? Poor old man!
I should have liked to have seen him once again!"

"Surely better not, Signor Marchese! What

would have been the good of seeing him only to
quarrel with him? Better as it is. Maybe he
never heard of your proscription!" said Sandro,
fishing again, for Casaloni had not said a word as
to being proscribed.

"Very possibly not!" replied he innocently;
"for news was always a long time in reaching the
Villa. But I don't see that it much matters whether
he heard of it or not, as it is!—Except, indeed,"
he added with a sigh, "that, if he never heard of
it, he would have been spared an additional pang of
sorrow."

"Well, I don't quite see that," said Sandro;
"though, of course, you know your own affairs
best; but it seems to me that if he had heard of
it, it might have caused him to alter his testa-
mentary dispositions possibly."

"Ah! I never thought of that! And I don't
see now, as things are, how I am likely to find out
in a hurry whether he did so or not?"

"Do you know," asked Sandro, "whether he was
in frequent correspondence with his brother, Monsignore Casaloni, in Rome?"

"I rather think not! Not that, as far as I know,
there was any estrangement between them. But

the Marchese was not in frequent correspondence
with anybody.   He seemed never to wish to know
anything about anybody or anything five miles
away from Montamiata ! " returned the young man,
who, quite thrown off his guard by his companion's
apparently intimate knowledge of members of his
family, entirely forgot that the man he was talking
to was a perfect stranger, whose name even he did
not know.

"Well," said Vallardi, after a pause, during
which his mind had been actively busy with
sundry speculations and calculations ; " well, Signor Marchese, I have been thinking that perhaps
it may be in my power to ascertain for you how
matters have been left by the old Marchese in this
respect. And it is very desirable for you that you
should know."

"Really I am very much obliged to you for the
kind offer, but—you know, as I was saying just
now, I do not remember where I can have seen
you—and—excuse me, but—in fact, I do not know
at all whom I am speaking to," said Casaloni, with
the hesitation which a young man always feels in
similar circumstances.

"My name ! What, did I not mention it ? My

name is Sandro Vallardi,—a Tuscan! My acquaintanceship was mainly with Monsignore, the
Marchese's younger brother. He and I knew
each other very well many years ago. And I
have a very pleasant recollection of the matters in
which we were concerned to the mutual advantage
of both of us. By the way, what are your present
plans—for the immediate future—for to-morrow, I
mean?"

"Well, to tell the truth, signore, I have hardly
thought about that. I have had enough to think of
to get safe to the end of each hour, without caring
much for the one that was to come after! What
would you advise me to do?" said the young man,
with a young man's frankness.

"I should say that you could not have started
better than you have," answered Sandro. "The
Tuscan frontier is very near this; and when you
are once across it you will have no difficulty in
finding a safe hiding-place. The Grand Duke
doesn't want a larger share than he can help of the
curses the Pope gets so thick and hot from the
whole country. They won't give up any refugees
out of Tuscany, if they can help it. I wouldn't just
go straight to Florence, or even to Leghorn, or

Siena, if I was you. But if you want to keep out of the way for a while in Tuscany, nobody will be very sharp in looking after you."

"But how am I to get into Tuscany?" said Casaloni. "I have no knowledge whatever of the country. When I started from the coast, I thought it would be easy to find my way straight westward. But my experience of last night showed me that it was a great deal easier to lose it. And when I start away from this place, I shall have no more idea which way to turn my face than if I was in the middle of the sea!"

"Well, it is wild country enough here about, and no way less so between here and the frontier. But that is your safety!" said Vallardi.

"Ay! if I could only find my way through it," returned the other. "But suppose, after wandering all day, I should find myself back again close to Rimini!—and, for all I can see, that is just as likely as not. I suppose there is no danger to be feared from these poor devils here?"

"Well, I should be very sorry to trust them with my neck, if they knew a lira was to be got by twisting it, or giving it to somebody else to twist. And you may depend upon it they have a pretty fair idea of what has procured for them the honour of housing you!''

"No! you don't say so! What, these fellows living here in a hermitage on the top of this mountain?" cried Casaloni incredulously, and yet with some dismay.

"Bah! *Accidente* to their hermitage! You must remember that these fellows do not live like the Camaldolesi in our Tuscan hills, always abiding at the top of their own mountain, and really knowing nothing about what's going on in the world, any more than if they were in the moon. These brown animals go all over the country with their sacks over their broad lazy shoulders, begging from house to house, and carrying gossip from one farm to another; and then hearing all the news in the convents of their order in the towns, where they put up for the night. Lord bless you, they know all about the insurrection, and like enough were the first to put the *sbirri* up to the game. They know that the *giandarmi* are after the runaways, and, like enough, know the names and the *marks* of every man that is wanted. I should not wonder a bit if the old humbug they call the prior has got, in some pocket under his beastly old frock,

a note of your inches, and the colour of your eyes
and your beard!"

"And yet you said I had made a good start?"
remonstrated Casaloni, beginning to feel very un-
comfortable.

"And so you have. You are well on your way
to the frontier, and have got through the most
dangerous part of the country. And though I
think it very likely that you might have the *sbirri*
at the door of this den if you give these fellows
another four-and-twenty hours to sell you in, you
are safe enough for the night. It is many a long
mountain mile from here to the nearest police-
station. That is your safety. Not a man of the
lazy beggars will dream of turning out on such an
errand to-night. But you will see that one of them
will be off with the first light of the morning to-
morrow, and if you don't want to be caught you
had better be moving about the same time, and
just in the contrary direction."

"If I could only be sure of finding which direction that is, or of knowing at all which way I am
going," said the young proscript rather gloomily.

"Well, I have been thinking that perhaps I
might be able to help you," said Sandro, after a

pause, intended to give the young man time to dwell a little on the difficulties of his position, and to seem as if the speaker had to overcome considerable reluctance before he could make up his mind to incur the risk of so charitable an action. " I do not like," he continued, " meddling in these matters. I have learned by experience that it is best to leave them alone, as I was telling you just now. My affairs often take me into the Pope's country, and I might find it very awkward to have been engaged in helping to hide a man under proscription for rebellion. But, hang it! if one can never do a good turn to a fellow when he is down and hard-pressed, it would be a worse world to live in than it is! And, then, I knew your people, and should not be sorry to save the life of a Casaloni for the sake of old times. In short, I'll risk it, rather than see you come to grief, which you probably would if left to your own guidance. I'll see you safe across the frontier to-morrow morning."

An older man, and perhaps a wiser one, than Cesare Casaloni, or at least one possessed of a larger share of that narrow knowledge which is usually called knowledge of the world,—certainly such a man as Sandro Vallardi had been at the same age,

—would have felt some hesitation, under the circumstances, in trusting his life entirely in the hands of a perfect stranger, who might to all appearances have put a certain number of scudi in his pocket, and earned the reputation of a well-affected supporter of the Government, by simply guiding him across the country in one direction instead of the other. All that he knew in favour of the benevolent stranger was that he seemed acquainted with the names of his relatives,—people whose names and family relationships were well known to half the population of the Romagna. He had no possible means of guessing that there were very sufficient reasons why, even if his new friend had wished to betray him, Signor Sandro Vallardi could not have been tempted to put his own valuable person within reach of the Holy Father's *sbirri* by a very much larger sum than the poor proscript's betrayal would have been worth. For these quite major reasons, Casaloni was perfectly safe in his friend Sandro's hands. But the fact was no justification of his prudence in jumping at the offer without a shadow of misgiving as the young man did. But what a curmudgeon one would be, if one never trusted anybody save those whom it was prudent to trust!

"*O signore! Davvero lei è troppo buono!*" cried Cesare, jumping up and stretching out his hand to the older man, who still continued to lounge on his three chairs, and puff his cigar. "You will have saved my life; and you may depend on it, I shall never forget it. What name must I write in my heart, as that of the man to whom I owe most in the world?"

Sandro laughed a little laugh, which seemed half pleased and half cynical, and shrugged his shoulders, as he answered, "My name, signore, is Vallardi—Alessandro Vallardi. I am but a poor man, as you will see when you see me in my home;—a poorer man maybe than I should be, if all the people whom I have done as much and more for in my life, as I am going to do for you, had thought as much about it as you seem to do; —and had *remembered* their thoughts," he added with marked significance.

"I don't think you will find that I forget mine, Signor Vallardi," said Casaloni, "and——"

"Very good! I dare say you will not. Any way, I shall not remind you of them if you should forget all about it. Now, I am for bed. There are a couple of beds in that room there, and I dare

say we shall not disturb each other.   I suppose you
will be ready to be off at sun-rise?"

"To be sure!   The sooner the better for me.
Just give me a call as soon as you are stirring,
in case I should sleep heavy, for I am awfully
tired."

" All right; let's turn in at once," said Vallardi,
gathering himself up slowly, throwing the end of
his cigar into the fire, and filling himself a tumbler
of wine from the flask which had been brought for
the last comer.

CHAPTER IV.

A WALK ACROSS COUNTRY.

THE next morning Vallardi began, at all events, by being as good as his word. The younger of the two guests at the little mountain priory was still sleeping heavily, when the first rays of the sun rising from the Adriatic, whose blue expanse is visible by the eye ranging over all the extent of the city-studded low country, from that high mountain-top, struggled through the small and dim windows of their little dormitory.

Vallardi, who was well used to that reveillée shouted out to him—

"Hola! Signor Marchese! You are not in your chamber at the Villa Casaloni! *Tutt altro!* Up with you! It is time we were off, if we are not to let that smug-faced hypocrite, who wished us such pleasant dreams last night, get the start of us!"

In a very few minutes both men were ready for the road. Casaloni hardly noticed that his new friend had a short colloquy of a private nature apparently with the friar, who was called the superior of the little family. Possibly it might have excited his suspicion, if he had noted the circumstance. But though the few words exchanged between the friar and his guest were assuredly of a private nature, and could not have been spoken on the market-place at Rimini with advantage to either of them, they had in fact no reference to Casaloni in any way. And whatever ulterior views Sandro may have had, his present purpose was to bring the young man he had thus picked up, safely to the secure refuge of his own dwelling in the Maremma.

The trade of a conspirator and the lot of a detected one had appeared in very sombre colours to the young Marchese, as he had wandered, with little probability, as it seemed to him, of finding any shelter for his head for the night, over that bleak and desolate mountain on the previous evening. But now, everything wore a totally different aspect. The morning sun was shining gloriously, and tipping the already snow-capped tops of the highest ridge of the Apennine with gold in front of them. The air was deliciously crisp. The turf of the mountain-sides was stiff with rime; and the earth was sonorous under their tread. They swung along at a jolly pace, unharassed by uncertainty; for every step of the ground seemed to be, as in fact it was, perfectly well known to Vallardi.

"That is Pennabilli that you see there on that peak to the right," said he. "It is the last town in the territory of His Holiness the Pope; and you may swear that the inhabitants wish the frontier line passed on this side of their miserable little town, instead of on the other, let who would hold rule on the further side! We might pass by it, if we chose. But perhaps it will be better to give it the go by, and strike down the side of the hill on the left, which will bring us into the valley of a stream they call the Marechia. And then a very little more will put us beyond the frontier."

"Bravo! You seem to know the country well. I dare say you are a sportsman, and have beat every covert of it, before now!" said Casaloni cheerily.

"Yes! I know most of it pretty well; and have made a pretty fair bag not far from here before now," said Sandro with a peculiar smile, intended

apparently more for himself than for his companion.
"There are lots of custom-house stations here and
there along the frontier," he continued; "and those
who have anything on which they wish to pay duty,
make a point of passing by them. Others, to save
trouble, pass between them! I suppose you have
no special business to transact with the revenue
gentlemen, either Papal or Grand-Ducal?"

"Not I!" returned Casaloni with a gay laugh;
"and it would be a pity to trouble them for
nothing!"

"Quite so! We will leave the valley a little
before it passes the frontier, and strike over the
shoulder of the hill. I know a *contadino* whose house
is the first in Tuscany, and who will give us a bit
of bread and drink of wine without asking for a
lascia-passare. He has an unaccountable prejudice
against the *dogana* people."

"He is the sort of innkeeper for my money,
just at present!" said Casaloni; "and I don't care
how soon we fall in with him."

And with this sort of talk they beguiled the way,
while Sandro learned to form a shrewd notion of
the sort of man he had in his hands, till the frontier was safely passed, and the promised breakfast at

the free-trade-loving contadino's house had been found. And then, after a short halt, they started again. The worst part of their day's work, as far as mere fatigue was concerned, was yet to come. The main ridge of the Apennine, glistening with its line of snow, was still before them. And as Vallardi, professedly on his companion's account, but more possibly it may be suspected on his own, judged it still desirable to avoid any of the few and far-between roads that cross it, their walk over the top was a laborious one.

It was his intention to rest that night at another and much larger and better-known Franciscan convent among the mountains—that of La Vernia. They did not reach it till after nightfall; but found, when they did so, much better accommodation than they had been thankful to content themselves with the night before. Here, too, Vallardi seemed to be known, and though there was no avowed or open manifestation of acquaintanceship, it might have been observed that he was certainly no stranger.

The convent of La Vernia is situated also in a very solitary and dreary spot, on a very remarkable peak, or rather mass of isolated rocks rising precipi-

tously and to a great height above the other parts of
the ridge of the mountain. It is the ridge which
separates the valley of the infant Tiber from the
valley of the infant Arno. Our travellers had
crossed the former stream, and would have on the
morrow to cross the latter.

There is a numerous community of the children
of St. Francis at La Vernia,—a large and handsome
church,—innumerable chapels in all sorts of strange
places among the rocks, most of them with special
legends attached to them, marking them as the scenes
of some of the recorded incidents in the life of St.
Francis, and his personal contests with the fiend,—
a convenient *foresteria*, with good beds and good wine,
—a courteous welcome,—and no questions asked!

In this convenient and comfortable resting-place,
Casaloni and his new friend passed their second
night in that close fellowship which companionship
in travel, and especially in such travel as theirs,
brings about. They were by this time beginning
to know each other;—the younger man, it is true,
seeing so much of the surface of his companion only
as the latter chose to show him; while he was in
turn very thoroughly read and understood by the
older and more experienced Sandro. For Vallardi

was by no means the dull fool it pleased Il Gufone
in the pride of his own superior acuteness and alert-
ness of intellect to consider, and often to call him.
He was a naturally able man, whose life had made
him a practised and by no means contemptible pro-
ficient in the art of reading men,—the only subjects
of study his mind had been applied to. Casaloni and
he had found each other very tolerably pleasant
companions; though the nature of the two men was
as different as well could be, and their social status
and surroundings were separated by so very wide
an interval.

As to the impassableness of the barrier raised
between the two men by this interval, Englishmen,
to whose notions such a social separation would
appear insurmountable, would err greatly if they
applied ideas gathered from our own social condition
and rules to the case in question. A social outlaw,
such as Sandro Vallardi, part brigand, part smuggler,
and part freebooter, is figured forth to the English
mind in the semblance of some Bill Sykes, the
brutal ignorance of whose vulgar ruffianism is correctly symboled to the outer eye by unkemptness of
his shock head, the scowl of his low brow, the
dirtiness of his smock-frock or jacket, the ragged-

ness of his corduroy breeches, and the muddiness
of his nailed high-lows. While the young Marchese,
selected as the heir to the estates and representative
of the name of a great historic family, presents himself to the imagination in the guise of a young
gentleman of such culture, habits, and tastes as may
be expected to adorn the English occupier of such
a position. But neither prefigurement is correct.
And the incorrectness is so nearly equal in either
instance, that the social distance, which has to be
travelled over in order that the two types may meet,
is passed by a nearly equal departure from the
English standard in the case of the two Italians.
The Italian scoundrel is very far from being a mere
brutal ruffian as his English congener; and the
Italian nobleman is perhaps further still from the
cultured refinement of the English gentleman.

Two cultivated Englishmen would hardly be companions in a mountain walk for the duration of a
day without some such conversation as may be supposed entirely beyond the reach of such an one as
Sandro Vallardi. There is no reason to think that
such must needs have been the case between a couple
of young Roman nobles in the first quarter of the
nineteenth century. English gentlemen are not all

intellectual, it is true. But in the case of the most horsey and doggy squire, there would be discrepancies and incompatibilities of manners and of ways of living, which would render the close companionship of one very widely his social inferior disagreeable to him. And this, too, would be to a very much less degree the case between the two Italians. And this, it should be remembered, is a difference very much the creation of the outrunning of the southern nation by the northern in the course of the last hundred years or so. One can easily believe that a young Squire Western might have been well contented with society that would be very distasteful to young Western, his great-grandson, to whom Pall Mall is as familiar as any hedgerow on his own estate.

And half the distance, the annihilation of which enables the two men to meet, is, it must be remembered, annihilated in Italy by an advance from the blackguard side of the field. The Italian blackguard is not so superficially visible and palpable a blackguard as the British blackguard. Various causes contribute to this. Mainly this cause,—that no such general social reprobation weighs on him who lives at variance with the laws in Italy as makes

the English social rebel an outcast and a pariah.
And no such general reprobation weighs upon him
and completes his scoundrelism, because law and
social sentiment and opinion in Italy have for centuries been at odds.   Sandro Vallardi and Cesare
Casaloni, therefore, had been able to find each other
very tolerable company during their walk.   It was
an amusement to the elder man to observe the
unconscious self-exposition of the younger.   Sandro
judged him to be a weak, easy, good-natured fool,
whom he could turn round his finger at any time ;
and was rather disposed to like him withal in a sort
of idle way, as strong men often will feel towards
weak ones, whose weakness gives *them* no trouble.
The estimate was not very far wrong, yet not wholly
right.   Casaloni was not a fool.   Il Gufone would
have been competent to discover that he was not so.
But it was beyond Sandro.   The young man was
not only not a fool,—he had some of the proclivities
and tendencies of genius in him ; but they were
not sufficiently strongly developed, or planted in a
soil of sufficient richness, to produce any fruit of
value.   And the easy, good-natured, unstable weakness set down in Sandro's estimate was justly
charged enough.   He was one of those who wear

their hearts on their sleeves—a very un-Italian fault! And perhaps his practice formed no exception to the general rule, that people do not usually wear on their sleeves, or in any other similarly exposed position, articles of great value, or much worth the stealing.

Sandro Vallardi, on the other hand, was a very acceptable companion to Casaloni. There is always something agreeable to a young man in the conversation of those whose experiences, and consequent knowledge of life and the world, appear to them to be large. And of course the discovery that the experiences of the Bohemian department of life, however varied, render but a very meagre and stunted crop of any really large knowledge of the world, or of men and things, is the product of a later period of life. But there was also a vein of causticity and reckless cynicism in Sandro's talk and in his manner of viewing all things around him, that stirred the curiosity and excited the interest of Casaloni. He fancied he was listening to the somewhat bitter but wholesome teaching of an Ulysses, drawn from large and wide observation of the manners of many men, and the ways of a vast number of cities; while, in fact, he was being

regaled with the narrow and poor conceptions of a
scamp whose path of life had been through low valleys, whence no large or grand views of the higher
altitude and great upper table-lands of human
existence could possibly be obtained.

"If a poor devil like me," said Vallardi, on the
second day of their journey, as they were walking
down the hill from La Vernia into the valley of the
Arno,—"if such an one as I was to take a rifle on
his shoulder and turn out to upset the world, and
show those on the sunny side of the hedge that they
were not going to have it all their own way any
longer, I could understand it; though, for my own
part, I have seen a little too much of the world to
take any hand in the venture. That's not my way
of righting myself. But why such an one as you,
Signor Cesare, should not be content to let things
remain as they are I confess I can't understand.
But I suppose that you *did* find the life at the villa
with the old gentleman—*buon' anima !*—a little too
dull to bear. And you wanted anything for a
change, eh ? "

"Yes, it was dull enough, and no mistake! But
don't you think, Signor Sandro, that the object the
patriots had in view was a noble one ? " said Casa-

loni, anxious to place his own views of the matter and conduct in a favourable light.

"As for noble, you are a better judge than I, Signor Marchese, what is noble, and what isn't. I take it each man joined in the game because he was, for some reason or other, discontented to stay as he was. But, God bless you! you might be quite as sure before you began as now how it would end."

"Because we were betrayed, and——"

"Of course, because you were betrayed! And do you imagine that there was any chance that you should not be betrayed? Don't you think that every other man of the whole lot of you—ay, and a great many more than that—was quite ready to sell every man of you to the *sbirri* if he could see his way to a good price?"

"No! Believe it! No! And I would not believe it for all the world!" said Casaloni, flushing up.

"Very well! then keep off from believing it as long as you can, that's all! You'll come to believe it before you are as old as I am. Some would say that you ought to have learned that much already; and then you would have got something by joining the insurrection. As it is, I don't see that you are much the better for it."

"About that there is no mistake. I am ruined by it, root and branch. If I had stayed at home I should have been Marchese Casaloni now, master of the villa, and heaven knows how much else, and of myself into the bargain. And I would not swear that I should have ever joined the movement if the Marchese Adriano had died a month or so sooner than he did. But it is all up with me now."

"Well, that remains to be seen in time. But what do you mean to do now directly?"

"I don't know what on earth I can do," returned the young man with a sigh. "It is no use going to the villa; and it would never do to go to my father and mother in Rome."

"I should think not. And I should think that you would not be very welcome if you did. I take it that tender parents don't want to see much of their sons when they stand in your position. Why, it would simply bring ruin and destruction of the whole family, to say nothing of putting your own head straight into the noose!"

"I am sure I don't know where to go, or what is to become of me!" said the young man again, very disconsolately.

"Well, it seems to me that the best thing you can do would be to come home with me, and stay there for a while. You shall be welcome to the best I can give you. And I think I can guarantee that no *sbirri* will come to look after you there."

"*Davvero*, Signore Sandro, the offer is too good an one to be refused," said Cesare cordially. "I hardly know how to thank you as such kindness to a poor penniless proscript deserves. Perhaps the day *may* come when I may have it in my power to show you that I am not ungrateful."

"I dare say that that day may come, and then we will talk about that part of the subject. But, in the meantime, you must know what I have to offer you, and what you have to expect."

"If you will give me a shelter I can put my head under, Signor Sandro, and that, as you say, where no *sbirri* will come to drag me out from it, that is all I want, and more than I could have hoped to find; at all events, at the hands of one whom I had never seen a few hours ago," said Casaloni, with real emotion.

"All that you shall have, and something more; but not much more. The best of what I can offer you is thorough security. We don't see much of *sbirri, giandarmi,* and that sort of cattle, in the Maremma; and when they do come it's apt not to agree with them, somehow! You may stay on my rock above old Talamone as long as you like, without any mortal knowing where you are; and if you were never to leave it alive, nobody would be a bit the wiser. So you see that, if I am helping you, you are trusting me," added Sandro with a smile, that to some suspicious minds might not have had an altogether reassuring effect.

"All right," replied Cesare; "my life is not much worth taking by anybody, unless it were to sell it to the Government of our Holy Father the Pope. If you wanted it for any other purpose, I don't know that I should much mind your taking it."

"Thank you, I'll remind you of it if I ever want anything of that sort. Joking apart, though, I must tell you what sort of a place you are going to. I don't live in a villa like that under Montamiata."

"All the better, by Jove! I assure you I was desperately tired of that," laughed Cesare.

"Ay! but suppose mine is quite as dull without being as comfortable. What do you think, Signor Marchese, of living in a house where the only thing in the shape of a servant is a sort of hideous and

malicious goblin, who, if you tell him to black
your boots, is quite as likely as not to tell you to do
it for yourself; and by way of chamber service
might, if he was in the humour, dip your sheets in
the well, before making the bed? That is not quite
what you were used to at Villa Casaloni, I take it."

"Not exactly. There was nothing half so amusing
to break the dead monotony of the place. You can't
frighten me away from the capital offer you have
made me."

"Very good. There is my wife, who will do
what she can to make you comfortable. There
is the aforesaid goblin; and that is all, except
my child, a little girl—a mere child. Not another
soul will you see from week's end to week's end,
unless you go down the hill into the town, as they
call it—the town of Talamone, consisting of a dozen
or so of tumble-down huts of a few fishermen.
There will be a bed, bread and meat enough of some
sort, a glass of good wine, and that's all,—that and
safety."

"And what more can one want?" chimed in
Cesare.

"Well, some people do want a good deal more,
or else they make a deal of fuss and give them-

selves a precious deal of trouble for nothing," returned Sandro, with an approach to a sneer.

"I am not one of them. You will not find that I am difficult to content, Signor Sandro."

"Very well; then there's no more need be said on that subject.—Only, by-the-bye, I should tell you that I can't promise to stay at home to keep you company. My affairs often take me away. You must not mind me; but let me come and go as I like. My wife will do what she can to take care of you."

And so they journeyed on through the day, making quicker progress than they had done. For after they had crossed the Arno, Sandro did not seem to think it necessary to avoid the roads. That night they slept at the house of a friend of Vallardi's, at the bottom of the hill, on the top of which Siena stands. It was a queer sort of a lonely house, Cesare thought. No host was seen, and Sandro excused the fact by saying that he was away from home. There were beds, however, and a bit of supper for them; and for the third night Cesare slept well, sharing the chamber of his new friend.

On the next day Sandro again struck across the country. The road would have taken them through

the little town of Grosseto, the capital of the Maremma. But this Vallardi thought fit to avoid,
remarking that it was just as well not to let the
police people know that he was taking home a
stranger with him.

The country they traversed between Siena and
Talamone was very wild,—a tumbled sea of little
hills, among which wound a perfect labyrinth of
small valleys and streams. It was a district of a
character quite new to Cesare Casaloni, and one
across which it would have been almost impossible
for any but those thoroughly acquainted with
every part of it to find their way. Sandro, however, was evidently at home in every inch of it, and
brought his guest to his own door, before the sun
went down, without ever having passed through a
town or a village since he left the lone house at
which they had lodged the night before.

CHAPTER V.

"THE CONQUERING HERO COMES."

IT was not the usual habit of Sandro Vallardi to
vouchsafe any notice of his coming to the members
of his family in the lone house on the promontory
above Talamone. He might be expected at any
time to make his sudden appearance, and one day or
one hour was not more likely to be marked by his
arrival than another. It can hardly be said that
his coming was welcome to any one of the little
trio who composed the solitary family. The day
had been when his return had been looked forward
to by his pining wife as the hour for reaching
the expected well is looked forward to by a traveller
in the desert. His presence had been as the shining
of the sun to her. But those days were gone. As
continuous dropping will wear the hardest stone, so

will unkindness, if perseveringly enough continued, wear out, if not a woman's love, yet at least any active desire for the presence of that which comes but to bring suffering. Sandro Vallardi could no longer make sunshine in the house for Lucia. He came to her as to the others in that lone dwelling rather as the storm comes in a southern sky, sudden, overclouding all brightness, a cause of trouble to all and every one till it be overpast. To Leonora —now a lovely girl in the opening flower-time of her beauty—he was the least personally obnoxious. Although she, too, did not escape a stern word and look now and then, if she ever chanced to cross his will, he rarely went out of his way to be rude or unkind to her. But she could not escape from the feeling that there was a cloud over the house when he was present, and from being sensible of relief when it had passed away.

To poor Gufone the presence of his tyrant, whose servant he was not, not only because he received no wage for his services, was naturally no matter of rejoicing. During Vallardi's absence his life in the lone house had been as pleasant as anything the world was likely to offer to such as he. Easy or indeed little or no work, abundant food, warm shelter, kind treatment (for from Lucia he had never experienced aught else), the free woods to roam in, had made all that Il Gufone could want, or imagine that he wanted,—as long as these had made up the entirety of his life. Then of late years a new subject of interest and amusement had been added to his lot in the teaching and companionship of the child Leonora,—an addition that had made life seem to him quite surprisingly a matter of enjoyment; till all of a sudden a veil had been raised from before his eyes, as has been related, which allowed him to recognise this new element in his life as a curse and a misery, instead of a blessing and a joy, as he had imagined it to be. The coming of Vallardi, however, seemed but to make the suffering from this misery more acute, as it had before spoiled all the enjoyment. Besides, therefore, the ordinary allowance of cuffs and kicks, and jibes and snarls, and platters thrown at his head, and aggravated feelings but imperfectly soothed by railing in return, and by the perpetration of all the impish tricks his imagination could suggest, which the coming home of Vallardi brought with it, to Gufone it was unwelcome on yet other grounds.

Such was the ordinary state of things in Signor Sandro Vallardi's household.   But upon the present occasion his return home was attended by phenomena of a quite new and unprecedented sort.   The arrival of a stranger, and the sudden command that bed and board were to be forthwith prepared for the new-comer, was something quite out of the experience of any of the members of the family, and was an event calculated to interest all of them considerably in different ways.

The "differentia" of the stranger, as the logicians say,—the nature, quality, and kind of him,—were such as to enhance materially the amount of disturbance which his arrival was calculated to produce. The young Marchese Cesare Casaloni, notwithstanding those circumstances special to Italian society in that day, which tended to lessen the social distance between such as he and such as Sandro Vallardi, and which have been set forth in a previous chapter, belonged very evidently to a stratum of the social system very different from that to which Vallardi and his surroundings belonged.

Upon the host himself this circumstance appeared to make but small, if any, appreciable impression. There was a kind of rude and rough force about

Sandro Vallardi, a manifestation of strength not only of person, but of character also, which, in connection with the absence of any such moral characteristic on the part of his guest, and joined to the advantage of his superior age and the position in which he stood for the nonce, of host and protector to the younger man, enabled him to hold towards the latter a tone and manner of equality, if not even of superiority, as it seemed naturally and without effort. There was a kind of cynicism in his mind which assumed, with very tolerable success, a false semblance of dignity. Incapacity to respect anything played the part of the simple nobility of character that fails to recognise any inherent superiority in the mere external advantages of wealth and rank. His intercourse with the stranger within his gates was easy, unconstrained, and confined indeed, for the most part, to frank, convivial companionship during the hours passed together at table; for the presence of Casaloni did not cause any change in Vallardi's usual habits on the occasions of his generally short and far-between sojourns at home. And, upon the whole, he may be said to have taken but little notice of his visitor.

To the Signora Lucia the difference caused by the

stranger's presence was greater. In the beginning
it was a source of no little trouble and additional
weariness of spirit to her. She was, like Martha,
careful and troubled about many things, and per-
plexed by sundry difficulties in the carrying out of
the peremptory orders issued by her lord and
master. But by degrees she began to feel that
this stranger's arrival had been a good thing, and
his stay beneath her roof no inconsiderable blessing
to her. It acted, to begin with, clearly and to a
great degree as a check upon her husband's usual
brutality to her. It was impossible to behave before
a stranger, and a man, as Sandro was often in the
habit of behaving towards his wife. By degrees,
too, the presence of Cesare Casaloni began to be
recognised by Lucia as not only positively advantageous, but actively agreeable. He did not affect
any concealment from any member of the family as
to his real name, parentage, and position, or as to
the circumstances which had placed him in the
embarrassment in which Sandro had found him.
And his conversation, and the glimpses of the great
civilised world which it afforded her,—glimpses of
life, real, busy, moving life, beyond the dim horizon
of the farthest hills, beyond the limits of that dreary

Maremma, that had for so many long years been
Lucia's world, and her prison-house,—made a very
acceptable break in the terribly dismal monotony of
her life. And when, after a stay of a week or two,
Sandro again left home, merely saying, with reference
to the stranger, that he would remain there for the
present, and that he, Sandro, should probably be
back again before Casaloni would find it expedient
to change his quarters, and, coupling his careless
word of good-bye to his guest with a passing hint
that he would do wisely to abstain from showing
himself at Orbetello, or even at Talamone, more
than he could help,—when Sandro, without further
warning than these few words, once more took
himself off, Lucia grew to feel more than ever that
the having this stranger in her desolate home was
an alleviation, instead of an aggravation, of the
sorrows of her existence.

But it was to the two remaining members of the
family that the advent of Cesare made the greatest
and most notable difference. To Nanni Scocco,
Il Gufone, and to Leonora—Leonora Vallardi, as
she was presumed to be, and as Lucia had almost
come in reality to consider her—the coming of
this young stranger was indeed an epoch and an

event! It changed everything in the daily current of that monotonous life to one of them, and very many things to the other. To Leonora it was as the drawing up of the curtain which hangs between a child's eye and all the glories of the brightest scenic fairy-land. To Il Gufone it was the addition to his cup of life of a drop of gall so bitter that the entire draught was intensely flavoured with the bitterness.

Of course it could not be otherwise than that all this should be so. Cesare came to Leonora as Ferdinand came to Miranda! She had scarcely ever spoken to any man, had but rarely seen even any other man than her supposed father and Il Gufone. She had on not very frequent occasions, it is true, been down to Talamone, and had seen the human face divine, in such manifestations of it as the mingled influences of a seafaring life and a Maremma climate had there combined to produce. She had not, therefore, quite grown up in the belief that all the men in the world save her father were made in the likeness of Nanni Scocco. Nevertheless, it is not difficult to imagine that the coming of Cesare Casaloni was of the nature of a revelation to her. How could it be that she should do otherwise than mentally fall down and worship this Adam, so presented to her in her—in any similar sense—unpeopled Eden?

Of course also Cesare found, within five minutes of his arrival at Sandro Vallardi's dwelling, that the utterly unexpected presence in it of such a creature as Leonora made the prospect of his exile assume a very different appearance in his eyes to that which it had previously worn. Sandro, in speaking of the circumstances of the home to which he had invited him, while they were journeying together, had spoken of his "child" as a member of the family, but in such terms as had led Cesare to imagine that the "child" in question was little more than an infant. And it had been with an unconcealed start of pleasurable surprise that he had met the "child" who was to be one of the inmates of the same house with him for an indefinite but certainly considerable time to come.

It is not surprising that the whole aspect of his time of exile should have forthwith assumed a very different complexion in his eyes. Notwithstanding the genuine gratitude with which he had accepted the asylum proposed to him, and the real relief from very serious trouble which the offer had

brought with it, the prospect of spending at least
several weeks in a lone house in the Maremma,
with such society as his friend's description promised him, had seemed dreary and uninviting
enough.   But any number of weeks so spent in
company with the Eve thus carelessly assigned to
him as his companion in this lone Eden seemed
a vision of happiness.   The profounder the solitude,
the better !   Nobody to interfere with their com-
muning and companionship save the meek and
self-effacing Signora Lucia, and that half-human
animal, the Caliban of the enchanted island !   The
desolate Maremma promontory was converted into
a paradise forthwith.

And no sort of notion that any sentiments of this
kind were likely to arise in his heart, under the
circumstances made for him, seemed to suggest
itself to either Signor Vallardi or his wife.   Whether
the former were really blinded to the perception of
what must have been abundantly manifest to any
other mere looker-on at the circumstances of the
case, by his habit of considering Leonora as a mere
insignificant brat, or whether he had his own reasons
for choosing to be thus blinded, may perhaps be
doubted.   As for poor Signora Lucia, she had for

long years been too much crushed, and her mind too exclusively occupied with dwelling on her own sorrows and troubles, to be capable now of much active speculation or consideration of the affairs of others. Love had been for her too long a thing banished out of this her present world, and belonging only to times, places, and circumstances far distant from those around her, for her mind to initiate any notion that the divine presence could come into the immediate neighbourhood of her, there,—even there,— in that miserable, dreary home !

Cesare Casaloni, as the reader will have seen, is the "hero" of this our epos. But though not only the laws of art require, but the laws of nature also made it inevitable, that he should seem a very godlike and veritable hero in the eyes of Leonora, it is not necessary that any imposture on the subject should be attempted as regards the reader. Cesare had but little in him of the stuff of which heroes of the real genuine sort are made. He was handsome certainly, which is a great point,—handsome both in face and person. Had poor Gufone been as much so, he might have been the "hero" of the action. As it was, the notion would be absurd.

Nor was Cesare altogether without other gifts of the heroic sort. He had a certain warmth of imagination, which generally caused his first spontaneous inclinations to be generous, and his likings to lean towards what was good and noble. He had been capable of sufficient intelligence of the nature of the good things desired by the insurgents against the Papal government, and of sufficient desire that the lot of his fellow-creatures should be ameliorated, to induce him to join the movement in the absence of any very accurate conception of the risks of suffering which he was meeting, and in the presence of a very accurate conception of the exceeding dulness of life in Villa Casaloni. He had sufficient power of intelligence and elevation of sentiment to comprehend and admire the great poets of his own language, and to aspire to being——he also ——a poet. He was quite as brave as most men are, being ready enough to meet anything disagreeable for a cause, or a thing, or a person he had at heart, provided the disagreeable to be encountered did not last too long. And he had the brave man's quality of not imagining that he was a bit braver than other men.

And surely here was more than enough to excuse

any Leonora for having placed him on the highest hero's pedestal her heart could imagine, even if he had been presented to her for selection among a considerable number of candidates for the post, instead of being invited to walk over the course, as he was, without a competitor. Such being his qualifications, indeed, it may perhaps be asked by other hero-worshippers of the sex most given to worship, what was there so deficient in my hero as to justify me in throwing doubts on the genuineness of his claims to the character? And, on looking closely into the matter, I think that the main disqualification consisted simply in this,—that Cesare Casaloni loved himself very considerably better than he loved, or ever could love, anybody else.

It may be thought, perhaps, that the absolute exclusion of him from all pretension to real genuine heroism on this ground is somewhat severe. And yet it may be taken for certain that Leonora, with all her inexperience, would not have set him up on a pedestal, and fallen down and worshipped him, had she been aware of that one fact.

CHAPTER VI.

A RAMBLE IN THE FOREST.

VERY soon the newness and strangeness of Cesare's domestication in the family of Vallardi began to wear off. Before the next departure of Sandro from home, he had, to all intents and purposes, become an accustomed member of the little family circle. The anxiety for news from the outside world, and especially for such tidings from Rome as might help to indicate how soon he might hope for a termination to his exile and his hiding, which had been the main interest of the fugitive's life at the time of his arrival at his place of refuge, ceased to occupy his mind. He no longer looked into the future, and speculated on the probable duration of his present mode of existence, but was perfectly contented with the life which each day brought him.

Leonora's long rambles among the surrounding woods, and even into more distant valleys, continued as before to make the principal and main feature of her life. How like her life was in its monotonous course to her former life before the great revolution, —before the lifting of the curtain that had revealed the new fairy-land glories to her! How like! and yet how utterly unlike!

A certain amount of change had come over the spirit and manner of those long rambles since the memorable occasion on which Leonora had first discovered that she preferred scrambling across the streams herself to permitting Il Gufone to carry her across in his arms. But the rambles had not ceased on that account; nor were they less infallibly made in the companionship and under the protection of Il Gufone. The difference in them, indeed, was for the most part only felt by him. And if Leonora was occasionally made aware, by some word or shade of behaviour on the part of her companion, that all was not between them exactly as it had been, she was far from understanding or guessing the meaning of it, and gave herself little or no trouble to discover it.

Did she understand the difference that had come

over her days now,—under the new circumstances,
when the long hours of rambling were shared by a
third? Unquestionably, she must have been conscious to the very bottom of her heart that everything she saw and everything she heard was changed
to her; that all the sights and all the sounds had
a new meaning and an expanded significance to
her; that there was a glamour over them all which
seemed to place them in a new relationship towards
her, and to give them new power of speaking to her
heart. Perhaps she was less aware that, whereas,
in the old days before the new revelation, she used
to return home tired, and, going to her bed after
supper, sleep the unbroken sleep of childhood till
the morning, now the night hours were many of
them spent in reviewing the incidents of the pre-
ceding day, in recalling words and tones, in recollecting looks and glances, in looking for latent mean-
ings, and in puzzled searchings for the explanation
of the wonderful phenomena which were developing
themselves around her.

The forest ramblings were now always shared by
a party of three. The first impulse of Il Gufone
had been to absent himself when he found that the
new-comer was to share in the privilege of accom-

panying Leonora, which had hitherto been all his
own.   But some feeling, which he did not trouble
himself with any attempt to analyse, interfered to
prevent this.   He could not bring himself to permit
Cesare and Leonora to wander through the woods
alone with each other.   No word said by either of
them had ever given him the right to say or think
that they would have preferred to do so.   But Il
Gufone had not the shadow of a doubt of their
feeling upon this subject.   And if repeated assertion
of the fact could avail to make it certain, it must
have been sure enough to his mind.   He repeated
the fact to himself over and over again while
writhing on his sleepless pallet.   For neither were
his days any longer followed by nights of tranquil
slumber.   They were nights such as Il Gufone would
not have in his moments of greatest irritation con-
demned even his tyrant Vallardi to pass,—nights of
intolerable bitterness and torment. . Each night he
swore to himself that he would no longer live in
the hell which his present life had become to him;
that he would not remain to witness every day what
it maddened him to see.   Yet each coming morning
found him again at the stake, in his usual place,
ready to take part in the excursion of the day.

The manner of Leonora towards him was perhaps a shade more frankly friendly and easy than it had been before. There was some unconscious feeling in her heart which caused it to be so! But this, too, to the poor Gufone, was no comfort, but, on the contrary, it grated on his sore heart as an additional cause of irritation and bitterness. For it only served to mark to him the more the difference—the immeasurable, the wide-world difference—in the relationship which, it seemed natural to Leonora, should exist between her and him, and that between her and the new-comer. Cesare, like a booby,—such boobies as lovers ofttimes are,—was sometimes jealous of the frank familiarity thus accorded by Leonora to her old friend, teacher, and companion. But Il Gufone, having the more lucid brain, understood better the meaning and value of such manifestations and shades of manner.

Of course the teachings,—the readings with her old instructor,—had been discontinued. Leonora had no inclination for the former studies. She was learning other lessons. And in truth, besides the lessons which Cesare was specially destined to teach her, his conversation was not without its improving effect upon her intelligence. He was, as has been said, a reader of the poets, not without tincture of poetical feeling and proclivities of mind. And though his intelligence was for every serious purpose a less robust and less acute one than that of the poor Gufone, and though he assuredly would never have had either the patience in labour or the capability of imparting to her the amount of instruction she had received from poor Nanni Scocco, yet his readings of the nature around them, and his renderings of all that the voices of the woods and the waters, and the skies and the earth, had to say to her, had an opening and widening effect upon her intelligence, and a charm for her, which made it seem that she was then able to know the fair world around her as it was, for the first time.

People often speak as if they suppose that the fear of the law is the main cause why men do not much more frequently raise murderous hands against their fellows. But apart from any fear of the vengeance of the law, and apart also from any reasoned or rational conviction of the sinfulness and inexpediency of murder, there is, I think, innate in the constitution of the human mind a very strong barrier against the commission of the crime of Cain. It is no doubt natural to a man to strike when he is angered. And a blow may kill. But I think that a man's mind has large tracts to traverse, and much instinctive repugnance to overcome, before he can determine on inflicting death on another.

Il Gufone, therefore, did not murder Cesare Casaloni. It would be difficult on any other theory to say why he did not do so. Fear of the vengeance of the law can hardly be supposed to have restrained him. There were occasions enough when he might have left him dead in the forest, and easily placed himself where the law would not have followed him. He was abundantly strong enough to have done the deed. And it is hardly to be supposed that human life had any such theoretical sanctity in the eyes of Nanni Scocco, or that his feelings were sufficiently regulated according to the principles of right and wrong, for him to have been withheld from the commission of it by scruples of conscience. It is certain that the prompting of sufficient hate was not wanting. Had a tiger sprung forth from the Maremma jungle, and torn the stranger limb from limb before his eyes, it may be assumed that the spectacle would not have been otherwise than a very pleasing one to Il Gufone. But he had not become himself a human tiger. In all the medita-

tions of his hate, it never occurred to him to take
thought to slay the object of his hatred. But how
bitter that hatred was, it is not difficult to understand.

It was intensified by Casaloni's conduct towards
the poor Gufone. It was not generous conduct ; and
it was assuredly not excusable on any of the grounds
that accounted for, at all events, if they did not
excuse, the hatred Nanni Scocco bore towards him.
Of course he could not suspect the unhappy,
hideously ugly Gufone of being his rival in the
affections of Leonora. But he could not forbear from
taunts and gibes directed mainly against poor Nanni's
personal deficiencies;—taunts and gibes uttered in
Leonora's presence, which, though, to do her justice,
she never joined in them, or rewarded them by her
smile or any other token of approval, she did not, as
it seemed to Nanni, resent as she might have done.
How could she resent anything from the new god of
her imagination ? She would try indeed to com-
pensate for such attacks and mortifications by little
manifestations of kindness and regard. But all this
served but little to salve the poor fellow's sore heart,
and not at all to moderate his hatred against the
offender.

It was, no doubt, true that Il Gufone did offend his handsome enemy. His presence was an offence. The old, familiar friendship between him and Leonora was an offence. His persevering attendance on their rambles over the country was a great offence. Casaloni would have so much preferred that these hours should have been passed *a quattro occhi*, as the Tuscan phrase is. Occasions were not wanting also on which some small share of the mortifications, which Casaloni heaped so abundantly on the head of Nanni Scocco, were repaid by Il Gufone. There were things which Il Gufone could do which the magnificent Cesare could not do, and things which the former knew of which the latter was ignorant. There were feats of strength and activity, for the display of which their wanderings by wood, and stream, and crag would sometimes offer an opportunity, which were as child's play to the long arms, sinewy legs, and rope-like muscles of the Gufone, but which the more luxuriously bred and more shapely limbs of the heir to all the Casaloni greatness could not accomplish. And such occasions were not a little disagreeable to the young Marchese.

It came to pass, therefore, that, although it could not be said of Cesare Casaloni that he hated Il

Gufone with anything like the same intensity with which Nanni hated him, it was certainly true that he had no kindly feeling towards him.

On one day it happened that Leonora and her two strangely assorted companions had wandered to a greater distance than usual from home. They were bound on a special excursion which had been planned by them for some days previously. Their object was to visit one of those wonderful dead cities of an extinct race, of which the Maremma contains so many examples, and which prove that the district must at one time, some two thousand years or so ago, have been as thickly populated and as thriving as it is now desolate and poverty-stricken. The proposition had come from Il Gufone, who knew well every hill and valley, and thicket and stream, of the surrounding country, and who knew also in a general way the meaning and the story of the mysterious names of huge walls and Titan-like fragments of the works of human hands, which are to be found hidden in the recesses of pathless forests by those who know where to look for them. Casaloni was not ignorant of the fact that the remains of Etruscan cities were to be met with in the Maremma, and was not insensible to the mysterious interest attaching to them, and to their power of appealing to the imagination. But Il Gufone knew the names and the localities of them, and was not wholly uninstructed as to the general notions respecting the vanished race, who raised them, which have been drawn from the study of them.

It was a beautiful day towards the latter end of November, about a fortnight after Vallardi had left the party of four in the lone house on the promontory above Talamone to their own devices. Perhaps November is the most beautiful month of the year in the Maremma. October may, perhaps, be called so in Italy generally. But in the Maremma October is not free from suspicion of malaria. And the autumnal beauties are still in November making that wild district look like a garden,—like an abandoned and uncared-for garden, it is true; but with all the wealth of colouring that under less mild skies is only rendered to labour. The scarlet berries of the arbutus are still making the hillsides glow in the sunshine; and the reds, the purples, the russets, the yellows, and every hue of orange and of gold, are decking the woods with such colouring as might drive a pre-Raphaelite to despair.

It was on a sunlit morning, one of the brightest
of this part of the year, that Leonora, with Cesare
and Il Gufone, started early on their expedition.
On this occasion, even if the Gufone would have
permitted them to go without him, they could not
have dispensed with his companionship; for he alone
knew the exact position of the place they wished
to find, and was alone capable of showing them
the way thither across the country. The place in
question might have been reached indeed, or nearly
reached, the greater part of the distance might
have been traversed, by roads and paths easy to
be found; but they must have thus made the distance very much greater. And such was not the
method of travel to which they were accustomed.
Il Gufone had no idea of traversing the country in
any other way than by as nearly following the way
"the crow flies" as possible; and he had educated
Leonora quite according to his own notions in this
respect.

The ancient walls they were bent on visiting are
not far from the town of Grosseto, the most considerable in all the Tuscan Maremma, and the high
road from Orbetello to the former city would have
been the more obvious route for them to traverse.

But the traditions which had formed Il Gufone were averse from needlessly approaching towns. And it made no part of his itinerary to touch Grosseto. Many valleys, with their respective streamlets, had to be crossed, and many low ridges of mostly wood-covered hill to be climbed and crossed, before Il Gufone pointed to a somewhat higher eminence in front of them, and told his companions that the ruined city they were in search of lay hidden amid the thicket on the top of that hill. So thick, so pathless, and so thorny are the thickets in question that it is by no means an easy task for a man to win his way through them; and it needed all the exertions of her two attendants to enable Leonora, little as she heeded such difficulties, to reach the walls.

They are a wonderful sight,—standing there nearly complete in their entire circuit, but enclosing nothing save an almost impenetrable wilderness of jungle and underwood, filling up thickly the interstices between forest trees of secular growth. Traces of routes, streets, or roads there are none, —no faintest vestige to be found. Yet other remains of similar cities show us with what a Titanic massiveness of workmanship roads and

streets must have been constructed. Nature, in
her long holiday time of some two thousand years,
has very completely regained her own. But not
in two thousand years has she been able to obli-
terate those giant walls. There they stand where
the strong hands of those unrecorded builders
placed them, each colossal stone in its place as
laid, uncemented and holding its own against
time by the sole sufficient force of its own weight!
Huge forest trees have profited by the uninter-
rupted secrecy of centuries to insinuate their roots
between the blocks of stone, even as they do in the
fissures of nature's rocks, and have become old and
enormous trees without displacing them. The
places where once there were gates in the walls
may be marked; but trace of the ways that led to
them there is none. All is now thickest jungle.
And malaria has in these days one of her most
inexpugnable homes where once was a busy and
flourishing city,—probably a port. For the sea is
at the distance of a few miles; fewer than now
separate Pisa from the coast; and Pisa was a
seaport within the historical period. The space
that now intervenes between this ancient Etruscan
city and the sea is exclusively composed of an

alluvial flat, stretching between the old Etruscan hill and the Mediterranean, and doubtless produced by the spreading out of the material which the streams have in the course of ages brought down from the Apennine. Doubtless also these operations of Nature, thus left to work her ends in her own fashion, without any control from the guiding hand of man, have produced the malaria, which now revenges man's neglect by rendering pestilential a district once studded by many cities.

CHAPTER VII.

A BUNCH OF ROSES AND A TOKEN.

THERE are in one place within the circuit of the walls some remains of the substructions of buildings. But it is doubtful whether they belong to the Etruscan period. It is difficult, indeed, to say when, why, or by whom the fragments still visible can have been built. They seem to be the remains of a half-filled cellar, with a small remaining portion of superstructure rising to some ten or twelve feet above the ground. A small portion of the arch which once covered the lower enclosed space, whatever it may have been, remains, and still forms a small amount of shelter,—if any creature save wild boar or wolf can be supposed to have ever had any need of shelter there. There stands this last remaining fragment of a great city,—if, indeed,

it be not the work of some long subsequent period,
—meaningless in the very thickest of the thick
wood. Meaningless, but not without beauty; for
nature can always achieve that by herself. She will
not fit the world for man's uses without aid from
the labour of man's hands. But even though she
be, when left to her own devices, elaborating death
for the race of man, she never fails in producing that
which is beautiful to his eye.

And this lone fragment of the work of unknown
hands has been clothed by her with infinite beauty.
The grey of the stones, and the mellow red of the
old bricks, in their abundant setting of greenery
of every hue of the forest, from that of the young
fern, to that of the old ivy, and enamelled with wild
flowers, blended into a more cunning harmony of
colours than ever Indian weavers designed, are all
elements of, and ministers to, the sense of beauty.
The wild rose is not common in these forests; but
there are a few plants of it in this special locality,
as if they haunted the spot where man had last
lingered here. And one or two plants have thriven
wonderfully in the deep mould, the *débris* of hundreds
of generations of the vegetable world, heaped on the
débris of who knows how many generations of man!

The trio of explorers started, as fighting their
way through the tangled and thorny underwood,
they suddenly came upon the little ruin, struck
with the extreme beauty of the spot, and by the
unexpected apparition of these unobliterated traces
of man's presence in a wilderness where all else had
been so effectually obliterated.

Leonora, with an exclamation of delight, threw
herself on the ground at the foot of the old wall,
where there was a small extent of a few feet breadth
only of open turf between the ruin and the thicket.
Cesare Casaloni fell to poetising the occasion, in a
fashion that was really excusable, considering the
provocation. And Il Gufone busied himself with
carefully examining every foot of the remains.

"Somebody lived here once!" said he, returning
to the spot where Leonora was sitting, and where
Casaloni was pouring into her ear trite poeticalisms,
which to her had all the charm of novelty and the
power to excite her imagination. "Somebody lived
here once," said Il Gufone, speaking his truism
more to himself than to his companions.

" *O bello !*" exclaimed Cesare, with a sneer ; " Il
Gufone, after much thought and long examination,
has made a discovery ! Yes, my poor gnome !

there is reason to conclude that real human beings,
such as those you, not without wonder, see around
you, set up these stones and bricks once upon a time,
and lived here! Now it is better adapted as a home
for creatures of your species. *Non è vero, S'ora
Leonora ?*"

"The owls, he means, *Gufone mio!* Yes; it is
just a place for *i Gufi*, is it not?" said Leonora,
anxious to keep the peace, and to soften, as far as
in her lay, the insolence of Cesare's words.

"Ay! The *Gufi* and the *Gufoni* may find a
resting-place here now!" said poor Nanni, with a
sort of dreamy sadness. "But I am thinking that
those who lived here once upon a time, whoever
they may have been——"

"And you by some strange chance have learned
to read, and don't know that!" interrupted Cesare.
"I thought nobody was so ignorant as not to know
that these ruined cities were built by the Etruscans
—our forefathers."

"I do know, Signor Marchese, though I am but
one of the *popolaccio*, that the walls we have been
looking at were built by the Etruscans. Whether
they were our forefathers is another matter, of which,
I take it, your lordship knows as little as I. And

whether this bit of ruin was the work of Etruscan hands I very much doubt. But what I was thinking, Signora Leonora, when I said that somebody had lived here once, was that this place could not have been always as pestiferous with malaria as it is now; and I was thinking of the causes of the change."

"Is this a bad place, then, for malaria?" asked Cesare, looking up from the turf on which he was sitting by the side of Leonora, rather sharply.

"It is one of the worst spots in the Maremma," replied Il Gufone; "and a small opening in the thick wood like this is always the worst bit of the worst, for the opening teems with the bad air as a chimney reeks with smoke."

"What the devil then did you bring us here for, you evil-loving imp of the devil? If you knew——"

There came a dangerous look into the large red-rimmed eyes of Il Gufone for a moment or two, till catching the eye of Leonora with some expression in it which had power over him, he dropped his own to the ground at his feet, and said with slow and constrained words, keeping his eyes fixed on the turf the while, "I thought nobody was so ignorant as not to know that all danger from malaria is over at this time of the year,—especially after the rains have fallen ; and I am sure we have had enough of them lately ! You need not be afraid for your skin, Signor Marchese, valuable as it may be ! ”

“ I am not thinking of myself, *Gufo*, as you might have guessed, I should have thought, if you had any of the feelings of a man yourself ; but——”

“ Look ! ” cried Leonora, suddenly, feeling that some immediate diversion was necessary to avert an open outbreak of quarrel, “ look at that bunch of roses there, at the top of that tree ; ” pointing, as she spoke, to a remarkable cluster, which hung from the topmost sprig of a luxuriant plant that had clambered to the very top of a lofty pine ; “ who ever saw roses growing in such a place? And of course the finest are always the most out of reach ! I wish I could have that bunch of roses to carry home as a trophy of our day’s work ! ”

“ *Ecco un’ idea, come Lei stessa, tutta poesia !* ” cried Cesare, looking into Leonora’s eyes, as he reclined on the turf by her side, with enthusiastic effusion ; “ how I delight in an aspiration which can never content itself with any prize save the highest ! ”

Il Gufone was already stripping off his jacket. "You shall have the flowers, signora," he said, "if you have a fancy for them!" And without more ado he began to climb the long tapering trunk of the pine-tree by the process known to school-boys as "swarming up." His long sinewy limbs were admirably fitted for the operation; and he went up the tree almost with the facility of a monkey.

"What an animal it is!" said Cesare, stealing, as he spoke, a few inches nearer to the side of Leonora.

"He is a very good and faithful animal, the poor Gufone! And I love him very much. You should not tease him so, Signor Cesare!" returned Leonora, while an inexplicable sort of feeling began to steal over her, making her almost regret that she had sent her faithful squire on an errand that would detain him away from her side, overhead and out of ear-shot, for many minutes; although when she had spoken about the roses she had done so for the express purpose of making the opportunity for the little triumph for poor Gufone, which she well knew would result from the wish she had expressed, and which she had intended should help to soothe

the irritation and mortification caused by Casaloni's taunts.

"You should not tease him so, Signor Cesare, if you care so much as you always say you do to please me," said Leonora; and even as the words passed her lips, she seemed to herself to be afraid of the sound of them, and to be seized by some strange feeling of some sort, that made her wish that Il Gufone would be quick in the execution of his task.

"*If* I care!" said Cesare, insensibly lessening, by some writhing of his body as he lay on the turf, the distance of a few inches which separated his head from hers;—"*if* I care! Is it not the truth, Leonora, that you know at the bottom of your heart that I care for that more than for aught else in the world?"

Leonora could not abstain from darting one glance quick as a lightning flash from under the shelter of her long eyelashes at her companion, before she turned away her drooping head, with a movement that shook forward a wealth of long black silken hair, as a belle of the city might lower her veil. The abundant locks had hung loose, since throwing herself on the turf she had removed the large *contadina's* hat that had confined them.

"See!" she cried, suddenly clapping her hands, "he has almost reached the bunch of roses! Poor Gufone! he is at the very top of the tree!"

"I wish he would stay there!" cried Cesare.

"Stay there! on the top of that pine-tree!" cried Leonora with an affected non-apprehension of the gist of her companion's words, which was prompted by her own increasing embarrassment. "What has the poor Gufone ever done that you should wish such a wish?"

"Done! why he is always where he is not wanted! —always following you, as if he were a dog, instead of the stupid *Gufo* he is! If he stayed at the top of the tree, he would not be here, that is all! I never can find a moment to speak to you, Leonora; and—and I do so want to—to—oh, Leonora! don't you know what I have been so long waiting to tell you? Don't you know that I love you, Leonora, more—oh a thousand times more than I could tell you if I had from now till nightfall to talk to you without interruption?"

He had taken her hand in his; and though she still kept her face averted from him, she did not make any effort to withdraw it. But as he continued to pour into her ears his version of the same tale that had doubtless been often told in the same spot two thousand years ago, he essayed to insinuate his arm round her waist, as he sat beside her. But she frustrated the attempt by springing to her feet with the agility of a mountain kid; and shading her eyes with her hand, as she looked up into the pine-tree, where Nanni had not without difficulty just succeeded in securing the bunch of roses, cried aloud, "Bravo, bravo, Gufone! Take care! Take care how you come down! It looks very dangerous!"

"Take your time, man. Don't be in a hurry, or you may come down a great deal quicker than you went up!" shouted Cesare, who had sprung from the ground as she rose, and was now again standing close to her side.

"You are not angry with me, Leonora!" he whispered in her ear. "Is it so distasteful to you to be told that I love you? Leonora! I never loved any other! I never knew what it was to love, as the poets sing of love, till I saw you! Now I know it! Leonora, have you not guessed,—have you not known that all my life has come to be love for you? Can you give me no kind word, no kind look, in return for my heart—my whole heart, given to you for ever and ever? Leonora, will you say no word to me before the opportunity of doing so is gone?"

"Oh, Signor Cesare!" said Leonora, who had now withdrawn her gaze from Gufone in the tree, and was holding her face averted from her lover, with her eyes riveted on the ground, while her cheeks burned, and her heart beat wildly. "Oh, Signor Cesare!" she said, in a constrained voice, that seemed to his ears to have almost the tone of a sneer in it, "how can that be? How can you talk of giving your heart to me—to me, a poor *contadina*,—you who will go away as soon as the Pope will forgive you,—as father says he certainly will soon,—go away to be a marchese, and never think any more of the poor Maremma, or of any of the people in it!"

The tears had come into Leonora's eyes as she spoke thus; but she would not for a thousand worlds that Cesare should have guessed that they were there. And it was doubtless the effort to conceal all indication of that fact that caused her voice, unnaturally constrained, to sound as it did in his ear.

"Oh, Leonora! can you think of me so? You cannot mean it!" he said, still whispering in her ear, while his eye watched the progress of Il Gufone in his descent, to see how many minutes still remained to him. "It is true that sooner or later I shall doubtless be able to show myself at Rome, and that I shall have to leave the hospitable asylum where I have met with so much kindness. But forget it! never! Never while I have consciousness to remember anything. And forget you! Leonora, if you had ever loved, you would feel that what you are saying is an impossibility — a monstrosity! Leonora, either I shall win your love to bless and to make my entire life henceforward till life is over; or I go hence, not to forget, but to carry with me a broken heart—to go back to the world an outcast, with all life a dreary blank before me! Leonora, it is not the light love of an idle hour that I am offering you. Where is the man that could dare to speak to you in such a strain? I am laying at your feet the devotion of a life. Yes! I am to go back to be the representative of the honours of my house, and the owner of its possessions. But if you will not go with me, if you will not let my lot be yours, and my fortunes your fortunes, how infinitely rather would I forget, not the Maremma and the love I have there learned, but all the rest! How willingly would I pitch my tent among these forests, and forget

all else save you,—remember naught else, care for
naught else, and live only for love and for you,
Leonora! Leonora! For oh! I love—I love you
so much—so much, so wholly, so passionately, so
desperately, Leonora!"

Il Gufone was now swarming down the trunk of
the tree, and in a minute or two more would be
standing by their side. Leonora still held her down-
cast face averted from him; but he had again made
himself master of her hand, and he felt that it was
trembling in his. He had spoken with an energy
of passion which might have sufficed to charm a less
inexperienced ear than that of the young and utterly
guileless girl by his side, and might have moved to
love a heart less well inclined to give all itself in
return for that which was promised her.

He drew her gently towards him, and as he did
so he could hear the panting of her bosom, and see
the tremor which her emotion imparted to every
part of her person.

"Leonora!" he said hastily, whispering still more
lowly in her ear, "he will be here in an instant.
See, now, you shall give me a sign. I leave your
dear hand loose in mine. If you cannot love me—if
my love is distasteful to you—take your hand away.

But if there is hope for me—if you will not cast from you the devotion of a life—let it lie yet an instant in mine!"

The little trembling hand was not withdrawn. It trembled a little more than before; and the face was more completely averted from him than ever. But the hand lay unresistingly in his. And Casaloni knew that Leonora loved him.

In the next instant Il Gufone stood with his bunch of roses by her side.

CHAPTER VIII.

THE WALK HOME.

Poor Nanni Scocco was quite elated at the unusual warmth of approbation with which his hardly won offering of the bunch of roses was received by Leonora, and somewhat surprised at the increased degree of kindliness—or rather at the absence of marked rudeness—observable in the manner of Cesare towards him during their journey homewards. "Aux cœurs heureux les vertus sont faciles!" And Cesare Casaloni was very happy. As for Leonora, some other cause might perhaps be found to have contributed to the utterance of the voluble amount of thanks and praises with which she rewarded the poor Gufone's feat. She dwelt at length on all the circumstances connected with it, and chattered about it, and laughed, and called on Cesare to admire and

to applaud, till it seemed to Nanni that she was
making very much more of the matter than it deserved. And all this effusion was rather inexplicable
to him. The reader probably may understand it
better.

It was somewhat later than they had anticipated
when they left the old Cyclopian walls, and began
their walk homewards; and the rapidly decreasing
November days brought the sunset upon them
sooner than they had counted on. But there was
no great evil in this. The Gufone's knowledge
of the country was perfect. Light or dark, it was
all one to him. And there was much joking among
them as to the special adaptation of "Gufo" capa-
bilities to the occasion in hand. There was no
one to await their coming at home but the Signora
Lucia; and she was in nowise likely to trouble herself about their tarrying. Hours and their pro-
prieties were not much observed in the house of
Sandro Vallardi. And the Gufone and Leonora had
returned at all sorts of hours from too many a moonlight ramble for the Signora Lucia to be in any
alarm. The bread, the figs, the bit of " salame,"
the wine, that awaited them for their supper, would
be as good at one hour as another. And their

lateness, therefore, gave them no trouble at all. It was not likely that either Cesare or Leonora would find the walk too long; and as for the Gufone, another twelve hours of travel would have been nothing out of the common way to him.

Nevertheless, as the night was rapidly coming on, he thought that he might as well lead his companions homewards by a route that was somewhat shorter than that by which they had come. This track took them on one side of an isolated forest-covered hill, instead of on the other, and involved crossing a stream in a different place from that where they had crossed in the morning. The stream in question was one of several that had to be crossed in their way, but it was the only one that deserved the name of a river. Il Gufone would have made no difficulty of traversing it anywhere in its course, and would have thought it but too fortunate a chance had he been permitted to carry Leonora across or through it. But there was a bridge at the place at which they had crossed in the morning, and there was a bridge at the spot where Nanni intended them to pass on their return. And such means of crossing was the more needed in that the autumnal rains, which had been falling heavily within the last two or three days, had largely increased the volume of water which all the streams were carrying to the sea.

It was very nearly dark when they reached the place in question. The day ends, and the night begins, with very startling suddenness in these latitudes. There would be a moon somewhat later; but between its rising and the rapid setting of the sun there was a time of much darkness. There was nothing, however, to cause any difficulty in the crossing of the river. The bridge was but a foot-bridge, and a slender one of its sort,—simply a series of planks laid on posts driven into the bed of the stream. But there was also a hand-rail; and to no one of the trio did the crossing, even in the dark, suggest the slightest notion of difficulty or danger.

They came along talking and laughing, and without even making any remark on the river-passage before them. To walk along the planks with the assistance of the hand-rail, or even without it, was a matter that seemed to Leonora and the Gufone as simple as walking along any other path.

Leonora chanced to step upon the bridge first, and she walked along with a firm foot, still continuing the chatter, whatever it may have been, which had previously occupied her. Cesare was next to her, and proceeded to follow her.

"Stop, Signore Marchese!" said Il Gufone, putting his hand gently on Cesare's arm; "better let *la signorina* cross by herself."

But Casaloni, not understanding in the least what motive there could be for any such caution, and resenting his enemy's interference—specially his interference between him and Leonora—as an impertinence, shook off his hand angrily, and hastened with a quick step after the girl, offering her the quite unnecessary support and protection of his hand. In doing this, and in making as much as possible of the occasion, he passed her on the narrow bridge, and thus was first when they reached the centre of the stream together, while Il Gufone still remained watching them on the bank they had left.

A sudden short crack,—a great splash,—and a sharp cry from Leonora, reached his ears at the same moment; and in the next, with one bound, he was standing on the top of the upright post, from which one in the series of planks that formed the bridge had broken away, was holding the rail behind him with one hand, and with the

other hand and arm was drawing back Leonora,
already half immersed in the water, on to the plank
behind, which remained firm.

Exactly that had happened, the possibility of
which had led Il Gufone to recommend that Leonora should be allowed to cross the bridge alone:
the weight of the two persons together had been
too much for the old half-rotten plank, and it had
snapped in half suddenly, breaking off a little less
suddenly from its support on the posts on which
it had rested. The moment of time between the
snapping of the plank and its disruption from the
post sufficed to prevent Leonora from falling altogether into the water. But Cesare, who was in the
middle of the plank, fell head over ears into the full
current of the swollen stream. It was not more
than half a minute before the Gufone had placed
Leonora in complete safety on the firm plank behind
him. But Casaloni was in the darkness nowhere
visible. The turbid and swollen stream had already
carried him to some little distance below the bridge,
and it was clear enough that unless he were a swimmer, and a good one, or unless there were somebody
to swim for him, the Casaloni house and honours
would have to seek some other representative.

Cesare was no swimmer at all, as very few of his countrymen are; and his cries for help very plainly indicated to the two on the bridge his urgent need of it. Il Gufone had already finished his task of entirely securing the safety of Leonora,—not so entirely perhaps as to have made it certain that he had no intention of paying any heed to the drowning man's cries. But he certainly did not seem to show any such promptitude in hurrying to his rescue as he had exhibited in saving Leonora from the water; and it must be remembered that it is no easy task even for such a swimmer as Nanni Scocco was, to rescue a drowning man from a swiftly running stream, especially in the dark.

"Nanni!" said Leonora in a voice of intense entreaty, calling him by a name she rarely used, instead of his more familiar *sobriquet*, and placing her open hand on his breast as she spoke, "Nanni! save him! If you love me, save him!"

Il Gufone hesitated a moment, and Leonora again uttered the one word, "Nanni!" in a voice of agonized supplication.

"I *must* do it!" cried the poor gnome; and as he spoke dashed into the water, without even staying to take off his jacket, springing with a headlong

bound from the bridge as far as possible in the
direction of the drowning man's cry.

The darkness was too great for Leonora to see
either of the men, from the moment that Il Gufone
jumped from the bridge. She heard the voice of
Nanni, and once again that of Cesare; and then
for a few moments there was silence, and a dread
and agony such as Leonora had never guessed that
it was possible to feel before. Then came the voice
of the Gufone more clearly, calling to her evidently
from the bank of the stream, a little farther down
than the bridge. Leonora hastened to return to the
bank of the stream, and following it for a few yards,
found Casaloni lying on the bank, and Nanni kneel-
ing over him.

"Dead!" she shrieked. "Nanni! you have not
killed him? You have not let him be drowned,
Nanni!"

"No, Signora Leonora; I have done your bidding!
He is not drowned,—only half! He will recover.
I could not get him out quicker. It was no easy
job to do it at all!"

"But he seems dead! *O Dio mio!* Are you
sure, Nanni, that he is not dead?"

"He is not dead, nor dying, signora,—only

swooning; but I suppose he ought to have a doctor. These city signori are not as we are!"

"And where can we get a doctor! Oh, Nanni, what can we do?" cried Leonora, wringing her hands, yet infinitely comforted.

"We are not more than two miles or a little more from Grosseto. I could run there in twenty minutes, and fetch a doctor. There is none to be found nearer!" said Il Gufone in a slow and almost sulky tone, as if hardly reconciled to himself for having done as he had done.

"And will you run, *dear* Gufone, run as quick as ever you can, and bring a doctor? and I will stay here with him. Run quick, dear Gufone; and make the doctor come directly!" urged Leonora, clasping her hands.

"Yes, signora; I *must* do it! I will run! How fast do you think he would run to fetch a doctor to me to save my life? And I will tell the doctor that it is a *signore* that the *bella signora* who is waiting is so anxious about, and not such an one as the like of me; and that he must make all speed! Yes, I will be quick!"

And so the Gufone started on his two-mile run to Grosseto.

Leonora remained by the side of Cesare, who really might have been dead for any signs of life he gave appreciable to her ignorance. She knew, however, that in death the heart no longer beats, and that as long as it beats there is life; and, feeling sure that the form before her was unconscious, she strove to ascertain that the heart was beating still.

Gradually more warmth became perceptible in his body, and the breathing was stronger. Then the faintest tinge of colour became perceptible in the rising moonlight in his cheeks, and Leonora, with a strange mixture of conflicting feelings, began almost to fear that her patient would recover complete consciousness before the doctor's arrival. She would fain that he should recover, and remove the anxiety for him that still tormented her, as soon as possible. And yet she would much prefer that the doctor and Nanni should at their coming find her watching by the side of a swooning patient, rather than conversing with a restored one.

Il Gufone was not longer in reaching the neighbouring town than he had said that he would be. Nor was he long in finding a doctor, or, as fortune chanced, in inducing him to start on the errand proposed to him. He had been told that he should find the practitioner in question at a certain *café* which he was in the habit of frequenting in the evening. And there Il Gufone found him, and told him his errand, and induced him to come with him to the place where Cesare lay.

He had not remained in the *café* for this purpose above ten minutes; but when he left it with the doctor, an individual, who had been sitting by himself at one of the little marble tables that made the furniture of the place, got up and followed them. And as Nanni was leading his companion to the gate of the town, by which it was necessary for them to leave it, getting him to move on as quickly as he could, and telling him more particularly the nature of the accident which had occurred, the stranger following them put his hand on the shoulder of Il Gufone, whispering to him as he did so—

"Scusi, signore! One word with you."

Il Gufone, somewhat startled, and not being without reasons to dislike communications of such a nature, turned quickly, and saying to the doctor, "Go on, Signor Dottore, I will rejoin you before you reach the gate," eyed the stranger sharply, and waited to hear what he had to say.

"I only wanted to give you a friendly word of caution which may be useful to you," said the stranger. "Your grandfather, that you ran away from eight years ago, has found out where you are; and if you don't wish to have to return to him, you had better make the best of your way out of this neighbourhood."

Nanni Scocco started violently, and looked hard into the stranger's face. He could not remember that he had ever seen the man before; and for a minute or so he seemed to be altogether taken aback by the sudden communication. But he very soon recovered his presence of mind and the quietude of manner which made him seem a very different person when he was, as now, among strangers, to what he appeared when repelling and returning Sandro Vallardi's taunts and gibes at home.

"Thank you, signore," he said, "I am obliged to you, if you mean me well. But there is no necessity for me to avoid my grandfather or anybody he may send after me now. I was a boy when I ran away from him. I am a man now. Nobody has any right to compel me to go hither or thither, or to live anywhere save where I choose."

"That is all quite true, Signor Nanni Scocco,"

returned the stranger, " quite true and aboveboard ; and there is no reason why I should not be equally candid with you. My only object in addressing you as I did was to ascertain that you were indeed the Nanni Scocco who ran away from the roof of your grandfather, the Arcidosso Sacristan, about eight years ago. You admit that you are the same. That is all I want. Excuse me for interrupting you, and good night. *A rivedirci !* "

" Stay one minute, signore," said Nanni ; " only one word. Have you any objection to tell me also why you wanted to know what you have found out, and how you came to know anything about so poor a poor devil as I am ?"

" On those points, Signor Scocco, you must excuse me for the present," returned the stranger ; " and, once more, permit me to say *Addio !* and *A rivedirci !* "

" *A rivedirci !*" muttered Nanni, as he hastened to follow the doctor. " *A rivedirci !* I am not so sure of that. Who on earth can the man be, and what can he want with me? Well, any way I am my own master at last, and it doesn't matter much. But I should have liked to know whether the old man is still alive or not."

And so, muttering and thinking, Il Gufone over-took the doctor; and at the end of somewhat more than an hour from the time that he had left Leonora and Cesare on the bank of the unlucky stream, he succeeded in conducting him to his patient.

Cesare had already so far recovered from his half drowning as to have been able to speak a few words, to Leonora's infinite delight. Nor was it less delicious to her to hear that his first half-wan-dering words had reference to her and her safety. She need not, however, have troubled herself with any apprehensions that Nanni and the doctor would find her and Cesare in the enjoyment of a lovers' moonlight *tête-à-tête*. They had neither of them the least appearance of anything of the kind. Cesare was still far from thoroughly recovered; and Leonora, drenched to the skin, though in reality not much the worse for her drenching, presented a not much less woe-begone appearance.

It was not long, however, before the application of the stimulants, with which the doctor had come provided, produced such a restorative effect upon Casaloni, that he was able, with the assistance of his companions, to attempt setting out on his way homewards. It was a somewhat tedious and lonesome march that they made of it. But it is not probable that either Cesare or Leonora ever had during the remainder of their lives any nearly so delightful a walk again.

The lone house on the promontory above Tala-mone was reached at last. The story of their adventure was told to Signora Lucia. The frugal supper was eaten; and each, except poor Signora Lucia, who had no idea of anything of the kind, when they went to their rest, knew as much of the state of their respective feelings as the others could have told them. Leonora knew that she was loved; Cesare, that he had won all her heart in return for his love; and enough had transpired to leave the Gufone in no ignorance as to these facts. It is needless to attempt to picture the immense happiness of the two fortunate ones, or to describe the gilded dreams which, in waking or in sleeping, were theirs. Such dreamings are comprehensible enough to all, but can be described by none.

The state of the poor Gufo's mind can also be understood or guessed by the reader—not by either of his companions; for the general knowledge of what each was feeling did not extend to the in-spection by either of the others of anything that so little invited looking into as the heart of the Gufone. And neither to Cesare nor to Leonora did it occur to dream that the love which he bore her was as a fire of straw compared to the ardent passion of affection which poor Nanni Scocco concealed in his secret breast for the girl whom he had watched growing into loveliness beneath his eye and beneath his care.

CHAPTER IX.

" GOOD-BYE, SWEETHEART, GOOD-BYE ! "

THE quiet, monotonous life in Sandro Vallardi's house went on from day to day, in the prolonged absence of its master, much the same, to all outward appearance, after the memorable visit to the ruined Etruscan city as before. Nevertheless, to those of the little party of four who inhabited it there was a difference which changed the whole colour and flavour of their lives. Leonora and Cesare had recognised the fact, and admitted, that their mutual affection made them all in all to each other. Of course their lives and all the world around them become forthwith glorified, even as are the hills and the woods and the fields when the all-gilding sun rises on them. Most of those whose eyes will rest on these pages will know and understand this;

and for those who do not understand it, let us hope that they shortly may. The case was a normal and every-day one.

But the case of the poor Gufone was a less simple matter. Of course the state of things between Cesare and Leonora was no secret to him. They did not affect to make any secret of it. Leonora's mother—as she imagined her to be—was fully aware of it, and rejoiced with a joy that almost seemed to cast a gleam of brightness over her own pale and colourless life at the happiness and good fortune of the girl whom she had almost come to consider as a daughter. The lovers made no secret of their happiness; but had they striven ever so much to do so, they could not have eluded the observation of Il Gufone, sharpened as it was by the sense of his own misery and an utterly hopeless, all-consuming jealousy. It was hardly possible that he could imagine that Cesare Casaloni had taken from him that which, but for the stranger's coming, might have been his. He must have felt that, had no such incident as Cesare's coming among them ever happened, still there would have been no hope for him. Men are often to a wonderful extent capable of deceiving themselves in such matters.

But Nanni Scocco was not one of them. He had a large allotment of the unhappy gift of self-knowledge; and it told him that, under no circumstances, could the love of Leonora have been his. But this consciousness did not avail to make Casaloni less hateful to him, or to diminish the weight of his own wretchedness. Had he looked up to his happy rival with any of that respect which the recognition of high qualities, however unwillingly accorded, compels, the spectacle of the love of Leonora and Cesare would have been less wholly odious to him. But he recognised no superiority in Casaloni over himself in any other quality save that of external beauty. He judged him to be weak, unstable, and selfish, and was fully persuaded that the day would come when Leonora's love would be a curse and a misery instead of a blessing and a happiness to her. Cesare was the possessor of some accomplishments which the poor vagabond Gufone could lay no claim to. But they were not such as moved the envy or won the high opinion of the latter, who was conscious that his own native intelligence was a larger and stronger one than that of the young Marchese.

In a word, it was all bitterness, gall, difficulty,

repressed irritation, and daily and nightly misery to
poor Nanni Scocco. And if it had not been that
some invincible attraction, against which he struggled
in vain, bound him despite himself to the spot,—
bound him writhing as he was to the stake at which
he was suffering his martyrdom,—he would have
fled from the place at all hazards.

Thus the days grew into weeks, and the weeks
into months, and the autumn became winter; and
though the Maremma was still green in its valleys,
and brown on its hills, the distant Apennine chain
was white with snow.

At length one fine bright morning, about the
middle of December, Sandro Vallardi made his
appearance. As usual, he came quite unexpectedly,
without any word of warning; and, as was not so
usual with him, apparently in very good humour.
It was a short time before the hour of the mid-day
meal that he lifted the latch and entered the
door; and all the four inmates of the house were
assembled in the large living and eating room on
which the outer door opened. Cesare and Leonora
were sitting together on a settle on one side of the
huge hearth; Signora Lucia was standing over
the glowing ashes of a large wood fire, busied with

some culinary preparation for the mid-day meal; and Il Gufone was engaged in placing plates and knives and forks, and bread and wine, upon the table, already covered with its clean whitey-brown hempen cloth.

With one sharp glance Sandro noted the position and occupations of them all, and gave to each a gracious nod of salutation.

"Glad to see that you are cooking, Lucia, for I am as hungry as a famished wolf! *Buon giorno!* Signore Cesare. No news from home yet, eh? Well, I don't think that you will be much longer without it. Why, Gufone, what is the matter with you? You look as if you had been bled every day for a month past, till there was not a drop of blood left in your body. You are losing your beauty altogether. Isn't he, Leonora? I have left you at home too long. I hope you are all ready for your dinner, for I don't care how soon we get it!"

After the meal was over Sandro left the table, and went up-stairs, giving his wife, as he passed her, a look which conveyed his orders that she should follow him.

"Has that youngster been making a fool of that

girl down-stairs?" he asked of his wife, as soon as they were together in the privacy of the up-stairs chamber; "it looks to me very like it. He won't be here much longer."

Then Lucia told him how matters had gone between Cesare and Leonora, and explained to him that they considered themselves engaged to each other; and that Casaloni's departure, if, as she hoped, it would be caused by the circumstance of his pardon having been obtained from the Papal government, would doubtless have the result of removing all impediment to an immediate marriage between them.

" It is perfectly wonderful," said Sandro, with a long sigh, "what fools women are when there is any matter of marriage in question. Why, how can you imagine it a likely thing that this young Marchese is going to marry a girl in the position of your daughter? I wonder you have not more common sense!"

"But, Sandro, in the first place, she is not our daughter, you know; and——"

"Have not I told you that that is a subject on which you are never to open your mouth?"

"But to you, Sandro——"

"Not even to me! I suppose you have never done so to anybody else?" said he, fiercely.

"Never, Sandro! I have never opened my lips to any living soul——"

"Not to the girl herself, or to that young Marchese there?"

"Never! why, I never even think of it; I had almost forgotten it, Sandro!"

"Bah! what fools women are, to be sure! Don't forget it! Maybe the time is coming near when you may have to remember it after all these years!"

"Remember what, Sandro?" asked his wife, looking up at him with a timid, frightened glance.

"Never mind,—nothing! Do you care to hear anything about your own child? or have you grown to consider this one your child so thoroughly that you don't care anything about your own, just for all the world as the hens and the cats do?"

"My own! my own little Stella! Oh, Sandro, if you have anything to tell me about her, tell me for mercy's sake! What is it, Sandro?"

"What do you care? I thought you had almost forgotten all about it!" sneered her husband.

"Oh, Sandro! I can see her now just as she was that miserable day that she went away! My beautiful baby! My own little Stella! Dear Sandro, do tell me what you have heard of her!"

"I have not only heard of her,—I have seen her!—but not, as you say, just as she was when she was sent from this to Florence,— nor anything at all like it. She is an exceedingly pretty girl, I can tell you."

"She was such a beauty when she was a baby! Oh, Sandro, might I see her? I can't tell you what I would give to see her!"

"Give what you would, you can't see her—just yet! Perhaps you may before long, if you continue to hold your tongue!"

"Where is the child, and what has become of her, Sandro? You will tell me that. She is my own child,—and you know that I shan't say a word without your leave!"

"Ye—s! I think I know that!" said Sandro, with a wicked smile on his still handsome face.——— "Well—the girl is in service in the Casentino, not far from Stia. Her master is a *fattore*, a rich man, and Stella waits upon his wife. They are kind to her, and she is well off, and well cared for. The hospital gave her the name of Ventuno;—she is called Stella Ventuno!"

" Ventuno ! what a queer name ! "

" Why, how do you think the hospital is to find names for them all ? So they call them anyway they can,—Ventuno.—Ventidue !—What does it signify ? "

" And she is well off, you say, dear Sandro ? "

" Yes, she is ! a precious deal better off than if I had let you keep her here ! "

To this the poor thoroughly cowed wife only replied by a deep and quivering sigh.

" There ! that's the way with you ! I thought to please you by giving you news of your child, and good news too !—But that's the way with you ! You hear that the child is well off, and well cared for, and you groan as if your heart was broken. Well, I've nothing more to tell you—for the present ! "

And so saying, Sandro left the room, and, sauntering down-stairs into the living-room, asked Casaloni, who was still sitting with Leonora by the chimney-corner, to come and take a stroll with him.

They went out together, and Sandro said no word to his companion of the conjectures his sharp glance had led him to form, and of which he had been so ready to speak to his wife. Neither did Casaloni say any word to him of his love for Leonora, as, supposing him to be her father, it might have been expected that he should do. The talk between the two men was mainly on the prospect of the young revolutionist obtaining a pardon, and being consequently able to quit his place of refuge and exile. Sandro did not profess to be able to give any special reason for the opinion he expressed, that Casaloni might soon hear news which would enable him to return to Rome. And it seemed possible enough that he might have formed it merely from such observation of the general aspect of public affairs as his recent wanderings, wherever they might have been, might have enabled him to make.

Nor did it ever occur to Cesare to imagine anything else, when two or three days afterwards the anticipations of Vallardi were fulfilled in this respect. One day on returning from Talamone, whither he had gone in the morning alone, Sandro produced a letter which he had received, he said, at the post-office, for his guest. It was from Cesare's father, announcing that a pardon had been obtained for him from the Papal government, by the in-

fluence of "the Marchese Ercole." The letter was
very short, and somewhat dry. The writer had evidently not yet pardoned the youthful ebullition of
dangerous patriotism, which had so seriously en-
dangered the future hopes of the Casaloni family,
and specially of that important scion of the name,
Cesare himself, even though the Holy Apostolical
court had done so. The young proscript, however,
paid but small attention to any such manifestation
of displeasure. The main point was that his father
informed him that he was free to return to Rome,
and was expected to make his appearance there at
an early day.

There was one other circumstance about the letter
which arrested the young man's attention, and somewhat puzzled him. His father spoke of "the Marchese Ercole," without any explanation of the style
and title so given to the younger brother of the late
Marchese Adriano. This ecclesiastical younger
brother had always hitherto been known as Monsignore Casaloni, a prelate of the Holy and Apostolic
Roman Court, high in favour of the Vatican, and
a likely candidate for a scarlet hat. What was
the meaning of this unexplained change of style in
speaking of him?

After a little consideration, too, Cesare was surprised that his father should have known where
to address a letter to him, as he had imagined that
the secret of his hiding-place was known only to
his host and the members of his host's family. But
this difficulty was removed by Vallardi's explanation
that, having been at Rome, he had been able to
ascertain that a pardon had been granted to
Casaloni and some few of his companions in the
late ill-starred attempt at insurrection, and had
thereupon judged that he was acting in the interest
of Cesare in letting his father know where he was
to be found.

Respecting the change made in the mode of
speaking of the Monsignore Casaloni, Vallardi professed to be unable to give him any information.
He strongly counselled his young friend, however,
to lose no time in starting for Rome, very cordially
and frankly apologising for his apparent want of
hospitality in urging his departure, and very
warmly assuring him that, were it not clearly his
own interest to show himself in Rome, nothing
would please him, Vallardi, better than that Cesare
should prolong his stay under his roof.

It was fixed, therefore, that Casaloni should start

for the Eternal City on the next day but one.
The young man pleaded for this one day of delay,
assigning as a reason for it the need of some preparation or other, which Vallardi knew very well
to be altogether frivolous, knowing equally well
the real motive of his desire for the delay.   But
he forbore from any remark on the subject.

That winter evening Cesare had another *téte-à-
téte* walk.   It was a bright cold moonlight night.
And while Sandro, after supper, sate himself down
by the ingle to finish the flask and smoke his cigar,
Cesare lounged to the door, giving Leonora a look
as he passed her, which very intelligibly asked her
to follow him.

They stepped out into the moonlight, and turning towards the woodland behind the house, strolled
towards that little summer-house on a jutting crag,
which Il Gufone had erected to do pleasure to Leonora.   The spot was a specially lovely one, com-
manding a wide view over the bay southwards as
far as the Monte Argentario, and out to the more
distant island of Giglio.   Now all was bathed in the
silver moonlight.   The lights in the little town
of Talamone twinkled far down beneath them on
the shore; but all around them was as still as if not

a creature had been breathing within a hundred miles of them.

They sat them down upon the poor Gufone's bench, and gazed out at the moonlight on the sea beneath them. Who does not know the subject of their discourse, and all that was said on either side ? Was it not, as the song says, " ever so, since summer first was leafy " ?

Cesare's first communication of the fact that he was to leave Talamone, and start for Rome, on the next day but one, seemed to Leonora to turn her heart to stone in her bosom ; it fell so heavy and so cold. Had she expected then, that the present state of things was to last for ever ? that life was to be a perpetual idyl, with Cesare and herself living without change from one day to another, like Adam, and Eve, with the lone house on the promontory for their Paradise ? Really it might have seemed so from her unreasonable dismay at the coming of the day she must have known was to come. Unreasonable ! Yes ; that is the fault into which ladies are apt to fall when they find themselves in the position of Leonora. Cesare told her, and tried to convince her, that she was unreasonable. But his arguments had no power to comfort her at all proportioned to their cogency. And then he found her more unreasonable; and then there were tears—many tears, and assurances, and promises, and lovers' oaths—very many oaths; and misgivings that no oaths could altogether quell; and lingering clingings, and hot kisses on wet cheeks; and mutual interchange of vows.

When at last they returned to the house, Leonora slipped across the big living-room to the stairs, and got away to her own little chamber, escaping the notice she had feared her swollen eyes and blistered cheeks might have occasioned, and spent the night-watches in extracting the best comfort she could from Cesare's reiterated assurances that he would return to claim her hand and her love as soon as ever he had ascertained his own position, and done what was necessary for securing his interests as the late Marchese's heir.

On the next day Sandro· told Il Gufone that he had occasion to send him to Rome, and that he had better travel thither in company with Signor Cesare. He delivered to him a sealed letter, with orders to present it with his own hand at the address written on it, "Al Stimatissimo Signor, il Signor Giuliano Batti, 16, Via del Fico, 3° Piano. Roma."

This was the sole business entrusted to him, and these were his only instructions. Having executed this order, he was to return forthwith to Talamone.

It is probable that both the young men would have much preferred journeying without the company of the other. But, for different reasons, neither of them thought fit to make any opposition to Vallardi's will upon the subject. And on the day that had been fixed for his departure, Cesare, attended by Nanni Scocco, set forth on his way to Rome.

BOOK III.

FAMILY POLITICS.

CHAPTER I.

ELENA TERRAROSSA.

THE sudden and unexpected death of the Marchese
Adriano Casaloni had brought about sundry modifi-
cations in the position and the policy of the Casaloni
family. When the late Marchese had sent for his
young kinsman, Cesare, and had informed him that
he was to be the heir of the family property and the
family honours, the step had been taken quite with
the consent and counsel of Monsignore Casaloni, the
prelate and expectant cardinal, his younger brother.
But then neither brother had expected that the
death of the elder was going to take place so soon.
Monsignore had imagined to himself his brother

living on to a good old age—till he himself should be an old man, and a cardinal into the bargain, and unfitted entirely, both by age and position, for assuming the position of head of the family. But now things were different. Now it was not out of the question that Monsignore might himself assume the position to which his birth entitled him, nor impossible that he might find such a change in his prospects and position preferable to a continuance of the career which he had hitherto pursued. No step had been taken by him which need render such a change impossible. Though a prelate, he had never taken other than deacon's orders; and the fact that one of the great Roman families found itself in the position in which the death of the Marchese Adriano placed that of Casaloni, was quite a sufficient ground for the seeking and obtaining by the next heir of a dispensation from all necessity of further pursuing the ecclesiastical career.

Perhaps, however, Monsignore Casaloni would have been content to abide by the arrangements which had been made by his brother, and to continue to look forward to a cardinal's hat, had he been left to decide the matter entirely according to his own lights and likings. But there was another person who had a very all-important interest in the matter, and to whom the death of the Marchese Adriano, with the attendant possibilities which have been explained, opened a hope and a prospect which had for long years been, not without terrible struggles and much bitterness, regarded as wholly impossible.

This person was the lady Elena Terrarossa.

The history of Elena Contessa Terrarossa had been a sad one; yet, perhaps, not more so than that of many, very many, another woman of noble rank, under the *régime* which southern manners, Catholic doctrine and practice, family pride, and poverty have combined to make for them. As a girl she had been married to a man old enough to be her father, whom she had never known, and scarcely ever seen. Of course, loving him was totally out of the question; but it was all according to rule. The marriage was in every respect a " convenable " one, and the conduct of the young bride was equally "convenable" during her years of marriage. Under the circumstances of her marriage the Contessa had been even more careful of her ways than the social laws prevailing around her had required of her to be. She had made a point of not suffering her house to

become the rendezvous of the *jeunesse* more or less
dorée of the Eternal City, or herself the object of
their leisure hours—their lives, that is to say—and
their attentions. But it would have been too much
to expect that the young Countess should live altogether as if she had been consigned to a nunnery
instead of to a husband. Some society was necessary to her. And no Mrs. Candour herself—
certainly no Roman Mrs. Candour—could so much
as hint an objection to the frequentation of the
Palazzo Terrarossa by visitors, the excellence of
whose objects, the sanctity of whose personal character, and the edifying advantages of whose society
were guaranteed by the all-justifying, all-answering
sacerdotal habit. Scandal is an eminently anti-
Catholic vice. Italian Candours are rare. Still,
as the old Conte Terrarossa grew to be paralytic,
while the Countess seemed to grow into fuller
beauty every day, it is possible that some barely
palpable filaments of gossip might have spun themselves round her name, if some idle and splendid
young member of the Holy Father's "Guardia
Nobile" had been seen continually frequenting the
Contessa's house at all sorts of hours. But an Abate
of similar years—a monsignore, however much "in

partibus " his see might have been—a young prelate
or two—*fi donc !*

Is it very wonderful if, under these circumstances,
no safeguard of shoe-buckles, knee-breeches and
black stockings, cassock and *petit collet*, availed
to prevent the young Countess from forming an
attachment, which was what the world and the
lady to her own heart called innocent as long as
her husband lived, but which very speedily lost
that character as soon as the death of the old Conte
Terrarossa came in time to remove its worse features
of gravity from his widow's fault.

Whatever degree of palliation for that fault can
be found in the permanent character of the tie which
bound the young widow to Monsignore Ercole Casaloni, *that* Elena Terrarossa was entitled to claim.   It
may be doubted, perhaps, whether the tie, permanent as it was and remained, continued very long to
be a tie of strong affection. It was one of the
abounding cases which everybody who has lived
with his eyes open can cite, to prove the nonsense
and falsity of the trash said or sung about " love
flying away at sight of mortal ties," and such like.
Love is very much more apt to fly away under the
pressure of all the troubles, annoyances, and humilia-

tions which arise from the absence of those "mortal ties" which society recommends and society's wife insists on.

It may be doubted, I say, whether the passion which had at first drawn the young prelate and the young Countess to each other continued in much force for a long time on either side. But the tie continued, and continued to be recognised by both of them. A child had been born to them, the Leonora with whom the reader has made acquaintance, and perhaps the first shock to the affection of the Countess Elena was caused by the necessity for parting with her child, which had to "fly away" for want of "mortal ties." But Elena Terrarossa was essentially a proud woman. And her pride moved her to feel and consider herself bound for ever to the man to whom she had voluntarily given herself. The world, perhaps, would have been less disposed to condemn and despise her if she had broken and abandoned the tie in question. And some proud people—or people who consider themselves and are considered such—would feel the interests of their pride best consulted by avoiding in any way the condemnation and contempt of the world. But Elena Terrarossa was prouder than those proud people, or her pride was of a different sort. For the contempt and condemnation which her pride felt it most painful to support, were those of her own heart and mind. So the Countess remained " attached " to Monsignore Casaloni.

As for that distinguished prelate and ornament of the apostolic Court himself, I think it probable that he would not have remained bound by the tie he had formed if he had dared, or had felt himself to be able, to break it. If he did not dare to do so, it must have been that he feared some evil would happen to him if he did take that step. And that evil could have been nothing more formidable than certain looks looked at him, and certain words spoken to him, by the woman he had loved, and who had loved him. It may seem strange that a Monsignore, and a prelate, wearing purple stockings and a straight-cut scarlet-bound coat, should have felt himself to be unable to face these words and looks. But so it was. Possibly it might have been otherwise if on any given day it had been made evident to the prelate that he must *that day* break with Elena Terrarossa or remain bound to her for the rest of his life. There is, we know, a courage to be found in desperation. But, on the

contrary, this breaking-off was a thing that could
be effected as well on Tuesday as on Monday; and
so it came to pass that it was never effected.

The necessities of the case, however, and of Monsignore Casaloni's position and future prospects,
had made it necessary that the connection between
him and the Countess should be jealously hidden
away from the eyes of men,—specially of all men
who in any degree aspired to the cardinalate, and of
their friends and dependants and spies. The Holy
Roman Court is probably the most efficient forcing
hot-bed in the world for the production of hatred,
malice, and all uncharitableness. Scarlet hats are
limited in number in this world; prelacies are not
really infinite; and the supply of preferment of all
kinds is not regulated by the demand. That which
is given to one man another cannot have. And the
first step towards getting anything for oneself is the
preventing another from obtaining it.

So that there were many men and many women
—for woman is man's helpmate even at Rome—
who would have been glad to spy and to have been
able to put their fingers demonstratively upon this
little flaw in the stainless respectability of a candidate for the purple. Caution, therefore, was requi-

site; and Monsignore Casaloni was very cautious.
The widowed Countess lived, as has been seen, in an
obscure dwelling at a distance from the palazzo
inhabited by the Monsignore, and all communication between them was managed with careful
precautions of secrecy. The Lady Elena never
went near the palazzo. Whatever meetings took
place between them were effected by the not very
numerous visits paid by Monsignore to the poor
terzo piano inhabited by the Countess. And these
were, for the most part, paid by the gentleman
in obedience to summonses received from the lady.

It was on the evening of a day not long after
the death of the Marchese Adriano Casaloni that
Monsignore was paying a visit to the Countess,
under these circumstances. The attempt at insurrection in the Romagna had just been discovered
and crushed: Rome was talking of the different
names which had been compromised by the movement; and our friend Cesare, as we know, was in
hiding and in love.

Though the weather was still warm on the coast
of the Maremma, it was beginning to be a little
nipping in the morning and the evening in the
streets and garrets of the Eternal City. But there

was no fire in the room in which the Countess Elena
received Monsignore. It was not altogether a garret;
there was a garret above it; and it was decently
furnished, not without some little attempt at elegance. The dwelling was not sordid, though the
house was a very poor one, and the staircase leading
to the upper floors of it a hideously dark and filthy
cavern. This mattered the less to the Contessa
Elena, in that she very rarely left the house. The
lady sat on one side of the fireless hearth with a
scaldino, or little earthenware pot of hot braise in
her hands; and Monsignore sat opposite to her with
a little table between them, muffled in his ample
cloak, with his large three-cornered hat on his head,
and the point of a neatly-shod and elegantly-shaped
foot, with a silver buckle on the instep, protruding
from beneath the heavy folds of his all-covering
mantle.

The Countess Elena was a tall, slender woman,
dressed in black from head to foot, with very considerable remains of great beauty. She had black
hair, a marble-white skin, bloodless cheeks, sharply-
cut, delicate features, too fleshless now for perfect
beauty; a lofty brow, a high slender nose, lovely
dark eyes, a well-shaped mouth, with lips too thin,

and perfect teeth ; long, white, slender hands, almost transparent, which the addition of a little flesh would have made beautiful ; and feet to match.

Monsignore, too, had been—indeed, most people would have said still was—a handsome man of that style of face which best answers to the epithet "comely." There was much expression in the face of Elena Terrarossa, and the capability of much more. But in the shapely features of Monsignore there was neither any expression, nor the capability of any. It was a placid, rather florid, oval face, with a pure white forehead, rather narrow and rather retreating ; hair once black, now iron grey ; well-marked and arched black eyebrows ; large, dark, placid bovine eyes ; well formed and rather, but not grossly, sensual mouth, and still brilliant teeth. He looked a good-natured and easy man as he was, who, as long as the world would provide him with a sufficiency of daily nutriment, and allow him to digest the same in peace and quietness, would give none of his fellow-creatures any trouble, and would prefer, for choice, that everybody else should be equally well cared for. He did, it is true, hate a little, in a quiet priestly way, those who were so grossly selfish as to wish to jostle him on the path

of preferment for the sake of their own ambition.
But even this natural sentiment did not move him
to any great excess of anger. He knew that evil
and turbulent passions are very bad for the health,
and need to be purged not only with fire perhaps in
a future state of existence, but also and more certainly with purgative waters, utterly subversive of
comfort and satisfaction, in this mortal and fleshly
life. And he eschewed all such accordingly.

"All that you say is true, *cara mia*, and very
important; indeed, I may say, of the greatest importance; but it is a matter which requires mature
reflection—very mature reflection. You will not
deny that it requires mature reflection!" said the
prelate to the lady, in continuation of their conversation.

"No doubt it requires reflection, Ercole," replied
the lady, not without some little shade of impatience and irritation in her tone; "of course, it
requires reflection; but I think that most of the
reflections which can influence the question are
reflections that you ought to have made many a
year ago."

"*Cara Elena*," began her companion, in a tone of
gentle deprecation. But he was not allowed to speak.

"Yes!" interrupted the lady, "I do think that the considerations which should regulate your conduct in this matter are such as ought to have been familiar to your mind for many a long year. You know what my life has been, and for whose sake it has been such as it has. And now—but, I do not mean, *mio caro Ercole*, to insinuate that you have not thought of all this. On the contrary, I am sure that it has been constantly in your mind. And I have no doubt—no doubt at all, that your own sense of what is right and due to me, and indeed to yourself, will lead you to take my view of the matter. But you are so apt to temporise. You let the days grow into weeks, and the weeks into months, and the months into years, and do nothing. Now this is a matter in which action, to be useful and judicious, should be prompt."

"That is quite true, Elena, if I decide—if we decide that any action in the matter is desirable. But——"

"Consider, Ercole, that it *is* decided. You know that it is so in your heart. You know that not only my happiness but the interest of the family requires that you should take this step."

"Still the purple——"

" Who knows if it will ever come ? The bird in the hand is worth, not two, but twenty in the bush, in this matter. You know how little can be built on court favour at Rome. And even if the Cardinalate were much more certain than it is, your proper position in the world is at the head of your family. It would be considered mere cowardice and sloth not to accept it. Make your demand for a dispensation at once. You know that there is no chance of any difficulty in obtaining it. There are too many who will be well pleased to see you removed from out of their path. Release yourself from the ties of your profession, do what I have so good a right to claim from you, and take, and let me take, our proper position in the world ! I have suffered very much, and very long, and very patiently, Ercole ! "

" I know it, Elena ! I know it ! But reproaches are useless ;—useless and—and—unpleasant," said Monsignore, moving uneasily in his chair.

" Nor have I the slightest intention of uttering any reproach ! I only mean to remind you of the past, as a spur to action, which shall lead to a different future. I am sure it is your wish to do me the justice, which is now, for the first time, in your

power. Have I ever complained of what was inevitable, Ercole? Have I ever wearied you with
asking for what it was out of your power to grant
me? But now—now, when this accident of your
brother's death opens the way to making everything right at last. Do you not feel that this
reparation is due to me, Ercole?"

"It is due! All that you say is true! Reparation is due to you, Elena! God knows I am
anxious to make it! But——"

"But what? What is the difficulty? What is
the thought in your mind that holds you back?"

"Well, I don't know,—I don't say that it holds
me back; but—what about this young Cesare, our
cousin? You know that——"

"Yes! I know that when it became evident that
your brother would leave no heirs, and it was considered desirable to settle the family succession, this
young man was sent for, and was given to understand that the family honours and property would
descend to him. But this was under very different
circumstances. This was when it was imagined that
your brother would live to an ordinary age, and
that at the time of his death you would already
have gained the object of your own and the family

ambition. Now this is all changed. The title and estates descend to you, and——"

"Stay, Elena!" said the prelate, interrupting, in his turn; "stay! it is necessary that you should understand the state of the case accurately. Certain lands, and unquestionably the title, descend to me. But a very large portion of the estates have been so settled on Cesare Casaloni, that they will indefeasibly go to him."

"And he a rebel, proscribed and in hiding! A very pretty arrangement you have made for the continuation of the family, truly!"

"Elena, the future cannot be judged of as the past can!" said the prelate, enunciating his bit of wisdom somewhat sententiously. "The premature death of my brother was not anticipated; still less so the culpable and lamentable folly of which our cousin has been guilty. But the latter is not irreparable. A pardon may be, and doubtless will be, obtained. He is young. He will doubtless make all submission. The owners of such a name, and especially of such a fortune as he is now the possessor of, are not the stuff out of which conspirators are made!"

"It seems to me that the more proper course

would be that his rebellion should be allowed to
become the means of undoing that which your
brother and you so imprudently did. Why should
not the estate be confiscated—he is a proscript—
and resettled on the rightful heir?"

"Such a course would appear very objectionable,
my dear Elena, to general opinion. I should be
very loth to adopt it. It will be a matter of course
that Cesare, making due submission, should be pardoned. Were his folly looked on in a more serious
light, think of the effect it would have on my own
career and on the family name! No! believe me,
that such a line as you have hinted at is not to be
thought of."

"Is the portion of the property which has been
settled on the young man large?" asked the
Countess, after a pause.

"It is very considerable,—certainly the larger
and principal portion of the family estates," replied
Monsignore; "unquestionably the larger part!" he
added, after a little thought.

There was a pause of some duration in the conversation. The Countess rose from her seat, and
walked once or twice from wall to wall of the small
chamber, while the prelate kept his seat, and eyed

her somewhat uneasily in her walk. Her pacing was not, however, a manifestation of passion, but of thought. As she stopped, tall and stately, managing the flowing folds of her ample dress as she moved with perfect skill and grace, the Countess Elena was meditating deeply.

CHAPTER II.

LADY AND PRIEST.

THERE was profound silence in the small chamber, while the prelate awaited, not without anxiety, the result of the lady's meditations. After some half-dozen turns she resumed her seat, but still did not speak immediately. One would have said that she too did not approach the subject that was in her thoughts without some show of misgiving and anxiety.

"I suppose that you are right, Ercole," she said at last, "and that it will not be wise to think of any change in the arrangements which have been made in favour of your cousin. But, Ercole——" she paused in her speech a minute, looking fixedly into the impassive face opposite to her, before she continued, "you have a daughter!"

The prelate started; and his placid, handsome face became flushed up to the roots of his iron-grey hair. For a minute he met the eye of his companion, but then quailing under it, he dropped his to the ground, as he replied:—

"I had,—we had a daughter, Elena; but she has gone from us, even as though she had gone to her grave."

"Ay! such, Ercole, was your purpose. I will not now say one word about the cruelty of it!—— not a word! But, Ercole, I was —I am—a mother, and I could not consent to such a purpose. I took means—broken down and half demented as I was by the agony of that time—I took the necessary means for securing the possibility of tracing the child at a future time."

"Heavens, Elena! the risk! think of the risk!" cried the prelate, evidently much, and not agreeably, disturbed.

"I took care, Ercole, that the risk should be little or none," said the Countess, with a touch of contempt in the expression of her voice. "Have I ever suffered any wish—any natural sentiment of mine to be the means of risking any of the things that you so dearly prize?"

"And——am I to understand that you are aware of where the child is now?" asked the prelate, with an uneasy anxiety, that almost amounted to alarm, in his manner.

"Yes, Ercole! I know where the child—child, indeed, hardly to be called any longer—I know where she is now. I have contrived to find the means of tracing her from the moment that she was torn from me to the present hour. I found the means of baffling your purpose of cutting off all possibility of communication, and all hope of ever undoing that which was then done,—and I still promise myself that you, Ercole, will yet bless the day that I did so baffle your purpose."

"I am—surprised!—very greatly surprised! All this comes upon me—quite in the manner of a surprise!" said the prelate, uneasily, and evidently very far from pleased by the intelligence communicated to him, but equally evidently too much in awe of his companion to manifest his displeasure in any very overt manner. He was, however, disturbed to such a degree, that he removed his large three-cornered hat from his head, and placing it on the little table beside him, wiped his smooth brow with a checked linen handkerchief

which he drew from his pocket. He replaced his
hat when he had deliberately done this, and had
folded up his handkerchief, and replaced it in his
pocket, and gathered his huge black cloth mantle
around him, without rising from his chair.

"Truly a surprise—a very great surprise, Elena!
and surprise is a bad counsellor. I know not what
to say. I fear me you have taken upon yourself
a very great responsibility, and—and—I am afraid
—an inconvenience!"

Again that expression of somewhat too clearly
expressed contempt came over the lady's features,
as, after looking at him for some moments in
silence, while she slowly nodded her head three or
four times, she said :—

"Of course, I know that you must be surprised, Ercole; and, of course, there is responsibility incurred; we will not stop now to inquire
when, or how it was first incurred, but I hope that
you will not find that the step I took will entail
any inconvenience, as you say, but I hope the
reverse."

"But, Elena, think of the risk! You must have
trusted others! It is bad to trust! always bad to
trust!" said the member of the sacerdotal aristo-

cracy, enunciating one of the maxims of his order
as a dictum of the profoundest wisdom.

"I trusted those, or one rather, whom I could
trust, and would trust again. I do not think that
it is always bad to trust. I trusted, and was in that
instance not deceived. The result is, that we have
still a daughter; that it is still in your power to
own her, and to rejoice in her as such; to restore
her to the position she ought to hold. Have the
possibility and the prospect of doing this no charm
for you, Ercole?"

"I am sure I should be very happy. I—
I—but you see, Elena—all this is a surprise—
quite a surprise! indeed, I may say, an utterly
unforeseen circumstance!" said the prelate, with an
air of wishing himself anywhere but where he was.

There were for an instant signs of coming storm
perceptible in the lady's brow and eye. But with
an effort she chased them, and suppressed the movement of mind which had caused them.

"I can understand, Ercole," she said, with
studied calmness, "that it must need some moments
of thought to accustom your mind to the contemplation of all the new possibilities which the
confession I have made to you opens before you.

But I cannot understand that you should hesitate about accepting them, or fail to see the great good fortune involved in them."

"But what is it you propose then, Elena? Let me hear clearly what is the course you would have me adopt," said Monsignore, with a tone and manner which would have enabled any shrewd by-stander at the interview to risk a heavy bet that he would end by acting as the lady would have him act.

"I would have you at once ask a dispensation, enabling you to quit the ecclesiastical career, on the ground of your brother's death having left you the natural head of the family. Under all the circumstances, you know that there would be no difficulty in obtaining this. I would have you legi-timatise in the face of the Church the union which has existed between us for now more than twenty years. How far I deserve this of you, you best know! I would have you—the Marchese Casaloni —recall, and own, in the face of the world, your daughter, thus * legitimatised and recognised as the heiress of the Casaloni name and fortune."

* Marriage at any period legitimatises offspring born previously to it, according to the Catholic Church, and the law in Catholic countries.

"But, Elena," said the prelate, who had been listening to this programme with all the faculties of his mind, "remember how poor a position has been made for any such heiress by the settlement of the family estates we were speaking of just now! Think whether it will be easy, or possible, to find such an establishment for—our daughter, as would befit her name and position, looking to the very restricted means that would remain to us."

"The principal part of the property goes to this Cesare Casaloni, you say. What I would propose would be a marriage between our daughter and this cousin. What could be in every way more fitting? The family property would thus be kept together, and the descent would remain direct in the elder branch of the family, through our child."

"Hum! Hum! Hum! Yes! The idea is not a bad one, Elena. There would be advantages in such a plan undeniably. I almost think ——But the young man! this Cesare, who has taken the bit between his teeth so much already, as we have seen!"

"This escapade of his might be made to assist our views. It will be easy for you to obtain his pardon. Would it be so difficult to cause it to be revoked?

Might it not be given conditionally? Might it not, at all events, be made to appear so to him? Would there, at all events, be any great difficulty in making him feel that it was in the power of you, the Marchese Casaloni, late Prelate of the Apostolic Palace, the head of his family, to make Rome too hot to hold him, late insurgent against the Papal Government, if you chose to do so?"

"Of that I think I may say there could certainly be no doubt," said the prelate, feeling the ground, with which he was well acquainted, safer under him.

"Well, then," continued the lady, "rightly managed, this pardoned young conspirator would be very much in your power. And what could he possibly desire better? His position would be made secure in every way. Though so much of the family property is his already, our daughter would not go to him empty-handed. He would surely see that the proposal was in every point of view one to be jumped at."

"And the child — our daughter? — Do you know — in fact, Elena — what do you know about her? What particulars have you been able to obtain respecting the child?"

"I have never seen her, of course, as you must know, Ercole," said the Contessa, with a deep sigh; "nor have I been able to hear of her often. This is what I have been able to learn. She did not remain with the wretched people to whom she was intrusted. It was well she did not; for the place to which she was taken was in the Tuscan Maremma, and God knows what would have happened to the child in such a place and in such hands. They did not keep her. She was sent to the hospital of the Innocenti at Florence; and happily—providentially, I may say—the people who sent her left with her the means of identifying the child; —probably their object was to have in their hands the possibility of exacting money from the child's parents, in case of their being able to discover who had placed the infant in their hands. Be this as it may, the means of identification were left with the child, and were carefully preserved by the people of the hospital, as is the practice there. The child lived and grew, despite all that causes so many— so many of them to die!"

"What is the child's name, Elena *mia*?" asked the father.

The mother looked at him with a peculiar expression of face for a minute, and shook her head sadly, before she answered him.

"The child has been called Stella. It is a pretty name. At least they did that for the poor foundling."

"Stella! It is a good name," said the prelate ; "and you know where she is now, you say?"

"Yes! thus also she has been more fortunate than could have been hoped. She has been placed with good and kindly people in the district the Tuscans call the Casentino. It is, I believe, the upper valley of the Arno. She is in the neighbourhood of a little town called Stia. I have been told, Ercole, that she is very, very pretty! Very pretty, and the people she is with, say very good, and very gentle! Oh, Ercole, does not your heart yearn to see her? Ah! how my eyes long to rest on her ;—my lost, my long-lost baby!"

"Certainly one must feel anxious to see the child. Personal appearance is of importance! If, in truth, this child is to be called to the destiny you have imagined for her, Elena, it is of importance to know what she looks like," said the prelate-father.

"Of course, instruction will be needed!" said the mother, speaking rapidly ; "she must be formed!

but that will be quickly done! No good would come of making her a prodigy of learning! If she has not all the instruction that one might wish ·in the first instance, that can be added afterwards. The main point at first will be to make her decently presentable in the world; and this will in all probability not be difficult. She comes of good blood! That makes all the difference! But oh, Ercole! how I long to see her!"

The conversation was carried on for a considerable time longer before the prelate and the Contessa separated. For it was necessary to go over the same ground several times, and to repeat the same arguments very often, before the slowly-moving mind of Monsignore Casaloni could become sufficiently accustomed to the new ideas to take them in. The interview ended, however, as it might have been foreseen that it would end, in the adoption of the lady's entire programme as she had developed it. By degrees she succeeded even in communicating her own views and feelings to her hearer so completely, as to make him quite eager for the realisation of them; and before he returned that night to the palazzo, all the details of the scheme had been settled between them.

The dispensation was applied for; and was granted, as a matter of course. The motive was one which is recognised by the authorities in those matters as a legitimate and sufficient one; and in the present case there was the additional facilitation arising from the exceeding readiness of many of those in high positions in the Papal Court to get rid of such a competitor in the path of their ambition as Monsignore Casaloni. The marriage was solemnised as soon as ever the late prelate was at liberty, very privately and quietly, but with every due formality, in the face of Mother Church; and a formal and legal recognition of "Stella Casaloni" as the daughter of the Marchese Ercole by his wife Elena was drawn up, and properly attested and registered.

And as soon as ever the preparatory formalities had been accomplished, Elena did not suffer an hour to be lost in recovering her child. A trusty messenger, armed with all the necessary documents and authorities, was despatched into the Casentino; and little Stella, utterly amazed, and scarcely comprehending what had happened, or what was going to happen to her, was taken away to Rome.

CHAPTER III.

CESARE AND HIS NEW RELATIVE.

CESARE CASALONI, on arriving at the last stage of
the journey between Civita Vecchia and the Eternal
City, separated himself from the companion who
had been provided for him. Neither of the young
men—one, probably, as little as the other—desired
to enter the gates of Rome in company with the
other. Cesare had been provided with a proper
pass. Il Gufone carried nothing of the kind;
but he had, doubtless, his own methods of finding
a *lascia passare* sufficiently authoritative for his purpose. The two young men had managed to travel
in peace and outward semblance of friendliness
together, notwithstanding the not very kindly
feelings that each of them entertained towards the
other. The hardest trial of the poor Gufo's for-

bearance, however, was, when at parting, Cesare would persist in charging him with all kinds of messages for Leonora.

"There is the post, Signore Marchese," he said doggedly; "I think you had better write what you have to say. I am bad at recollecting messages, —specially such as you are giving me. Two to one I should spoil them in delivering them to the signorina!"

"Very well, Gufo!" returned Cesare cheerily; "you can at least tell her that I shall not stay away long. I shall bring her my own messages soon. *A rivederci dunque a Talamone fra poco!*" he said, turning away to pursue his way.

Il Gufone purposed remaining where he was till near nightfall.

"Humph!" he muttered, looking after his late companion: "*a rivederci!* who knows? I should not be surprised if we never set eyes on each other any more; or not at Talamone, any way. Now, which should I like best—that that blockhead of a Marchese should behave like one of his own sort, and forget all about Leonora, and break her heart, or that he should be worth more than I take him to be, and come back to her? Which had I rather?

Ah—h! I know which I'd say this minute, if my saying would make or mar one way or the other! I'd bring him back to her, and then go and hang myself—I would! But which should I like best for my own self? Ah—h!"

Cesare, on reaching Rome, went straight to his father's house, and was received with no very warm manifestations of welcome or affection. He had expected this, and was not surprised at it. But what disturbed his complacency much more was, that his father seemed to speak of the pardon that had been accorded to him as not so certain and clear a matter as he had imagined it to be. All that was said upon the subject, however, was vague and uncertain. Either his father did not know, or did not choose to tell him, the state of the case accurately. All that he could learn with clear certainty was, that he must at once go to the palazzo of his cousin the Marchese, lately the Monsignore Casaloni. His father did not even think fit to mention to him the recent marriage of the Marchese Ercole, though he must have known that, preferring, apparently, to let him learn from his great relatives all that they had to tell, and chose to tell him.

It was late in the evening when he reached Rome; and it was settled that he should wait on the Marchese the first thing next morning.

It was about nine when he presented himself at the door of the palazzo; and at once perceived, from the manner of the porter, that he was expected.

It should be observed that Cesare was ignorant, not only as to how he stood in respect to the pardon of his late folly—such he was already inclined in his own heart to consider it—to be obtained from the government, but also as to his position with regard to the Casaloni heirship and estates. He knew that he had been named as the heir to the late Marchese. But whether any irrevocable step had been taken to make him such; or whether the late Marchese might have been moved to alter any such disposition in his favour in consequence of his late escapade; or whether it might be in the power of the present Marchese to place him in the same position he had held during the lifetime of the late Marchese, or to displace him from it; or, lastly, what the sentiments towards him of the present head of the family might be expected to be,—of all this he knew nothing.

Thus much only he knew, that it was not likely that a prelate of the Holy Palace would look with very indulgent eyes on such conduct as that of which he had recently been guilty. It was, therefore, not without a considerable feeling of uneasy anxiety that he awaited the coming interview, in a room of the first floor, or *piano nobile*, of the palazzo, into which he was shown immediately on presenting himself at the gate.

He had not waited long before the door of the room in which he was waiting was opened gently— not with any appearance of secrecy, but as by the hand of a gently-moving person—and a lady entered. Her appearance was such as very promptly brought Cesare to his feet from the chair into which he had thrown himself, and caused him to execute as profound and respectful a salutation as came within the limits of his accomplishments in that line. She was a tall, slight lady, eminently graceful in figure and carriage, dressed with perfect elegance, but with a total absence in the style of her toilette of any shade of coquetry or pretence of youthfulness. Her dress, indeed, was eminently becoming, but was almost severe in its grave richness. The pale face was one of very considerable beauty, and

she carried her small head—almost too small for her
height—on the long and slender column of her neck
with a stately and proud bearing, which was not
incompatible with a very winning sweetness of
expression when its owner wished to win.

The reader will have probably recognised the
late Contessa Elena Terrarossa, now Marchesa Elena
Casaloni; and had he seen her as she entered the
room where Cesare was waiting, he would have had
no difficulty in coming to the conclusion that it *was*
on this occasion her purpose to win the person she
addressed. Nothing could be more gracious, as well
as graceful, than the salutation with which she
returned his profound obeisance.

Considering all things, it will be admitted that the
position of the lady, and the errand which brought
her to that room, were calculated to make the interview she had determined on seeking a somewhat
difficult one. And a less proud and less self-reliant
nature might have sought to smooth away at least
some part of the difficulty by causing the young
man to be made aware of her coming, of her position, and of her wish to speak with him. The
Marchesa Elena, however, had preferred to trust for
the achievement of the purpose she had in hand

wholly to the resources of her own tact, talent, and powers of fascination. She was exactly one of those women who are able to exercise an almost irresistible influence on young men as much their juniors as Cesare was hers—who seem to them, in the beauty of their dignified and lovely matronhood, as Milman wrote of the Apollo, "too fair to worship, too divine to love."

Before she had opened her lips, the winning, on which she was undoubtedly bent, was already achieved.

She advanced with a sweet and welcoming smile towards him, and seating herself by the side of a small table in the centre of the little room, motioned to him to take the chair which stood on the other side of it. Cesare sat down fascinated as by the presence of a goddess. Had it been in any degree within the purpose of the Marchesa Elena to awaken in the young man any sentiment of the kind, I fear that no remembrance of Leonora would have availed to enable him to resist the glamour of the charm. Nothing, however, could be further from the lady's thoughts.

"Signor Cesare Casaloni," she said in a voice of great sweetness, "you know, of course, signore, that you have been expected here, and I am very glad that you have timed your first visit at so early. an hour."

"My father, signora, desired ———"

"Yes, it was at my special request, that he advised you to come to us early. For it occurred to me, Signor Cesare, that it might be well on many accounts that I should have the pleasure of making your acquaintance before your interview with my husband."

Cesare could not prevent himself from starting perceptibly as this announcement reached him. Of course, he had known of the life-long connection which had existed between his cousin, Monsignore Ercole Casaloni, and a mysterious lady, whom he had heard whisperingly mentioned as the Contessa Elena. So this, then, was that Contessa Elena; and the first use which his cousin had made of his lay liberty was to legitimatize the union which had so long secretly existed. A strange feeling of increased respect for this old monsignore cousin seemed to spring up in the young man's mind, as he looked at the Marchesa. It was impossible to regard a man, who had won and enjoyed the life-long love of such a woman, as altogether in the past as well as the present tense, a mere embodiment of old-fogyism.

The Marchesa perceived the little start, and understood the cause and the meaning of it almost as well as if Cesare had expressed aloud all that has here been explained of his feeling. But she did not allow him to be aware that she had noticed it.

Cesare bowed lowly in reply to her last words; and the lady continued, with a somewhat nearer approach to a frank smile on her beautiful lips and in her eyes, as she said :——

"I am afraid, Signor Cesare, that you may be looking forward to your first interview with the Marchese with some expectation that it may be an unpleasant one. You have been proving once and again, that old heads cannot be found on young shoulders! Is it not so? You see, I know all about it! You have caused quite a scandal in the family! But, perhaps, we women are better able, or more wont, to make allowances for youthful follies. And I thought that if I saw you, and made acquaintance with you, before you come to have your scolding from the Marchese, I might be able to make matters somewhat smoother."

"*Oh, Signora Marchesa! Ma Lei è troppo buona!*

ma proprio troppo buona! non so—I really do not
know how to tell you; how to put into words"—
And Cesare looked at the Marchesa as he spoke, with
an expression which very sufficiently assured the
lady that she had already very completely won the
victory she had come there to achieve, and that her
future plans would not be crossed by any great
difficulty, in turning this young man round her
finger, and making him do as she pleased.

"But you know," she continued, shaking her
head, as she looked at him with a smile in her eyes,
"that you come in the character of the prodigal son!
I hope that you feel all that is most in accordance
with that rôle! Because in that case, I do not
think there will be much difficulty about having
the fatted calf killed at once. You have had your
escapade! You don't want to play at hide-and-
seek with the *sbirri* in the mountains any more, do
you?"

The words conjured up in Cesare's mind a vivid
picture of his Maremma life, the lone house on the
promontory above Talamone, of Leonora, and his
forest and hill-side love-making. But there was
something in his heart that made him feel that
not for the world could he have confessed to the

noble and aristocratic lady before him any word
of this part of his hide-and-seek playing with the
sbirri.

"No, indeed, Signora Marchesa! I have seen
the error of my ways!" he said, attempting to take
the tone she had assumed; "and I cannot be too
thankful."

"I am glad of it! heartily glad to hear you
say so, my dear cousin! Why, how could you think
of such a thing? Conspiracy, insurrection, and
revolution,—*e che so io!* And you a Casaloni! Bah!
Trust me, my dear Cesare! all such things are a
losing game for people in our position, whatever
they may be for others; and a very unamusing game
too, when the novelty of it is a little worn off!"

"Believe me, Signora Marchesa, I know now how
true all you say is. But, if you could but know,
Signora Marchesa; if you could only guess how
deadly dull the life at the villa was, in the time of
the late Marchese,—*buon' anima sua!*"

The Marchesa Elena nodded, and smiled with a
look of perfect intelligence, as she replied :—

"I have no doubt of it. I can understand it all
perfectly well; and can comprehend that a young
man, with no sort of amusement, and no mode of

employing his activity, may be driven to any mad freak for a change, and for something of excitement. Oh, yes! It is very intelligible! and, as I have no doubt, the Marchese will agree with me in feeling, very pardonable. We must endeavour in future," she added, with a gay smile, "to make the old house a little less like a prison-house. Of course, you will let the Marchese see that you look upon your *escapade* as a mere young man's folly, and that there is no likelihood of your ever taking it into your head to meddle with any such mad schemes again. And, I suppose, I may say as much in your behalf."

"Oh, signora! it *would* be very kind of you. I should be,—I am so grateful to you."

"Because, you see, my dear Cesare, as the matter stands at present, you are here at Rome as it were on sufferance. Not that you are in any sort of danger of being molested in any way. But my husband has not been able to obtain, as yet, a complete and unconditional pardon from the government. I am sure, however, that it will all end without any further trouble. You have only to be a good boy, and fill the place the family intend you to fill well and creditably, and the conditional permission to return to Rome will very soon be changed into a complete pardon."

"How kind of you, signora, to interest yourself in the matter! I really do not know how to tell you ———"

"*Che! che!* What is there to tell? Surely it would be very strange if I did not interest myself in all that interests you! Are not our interests the same? What can either of us wish that the other should not wish! We ought to be, as I have no doubt we shall be, very good and close friends; and shall work together for the purpose, which ought to be the object of both of us, the establishment on a secure and satisfactory footing of the future position and fortune of the family."

"Ah, signora, with you for a guardian angel, the fortunes of the family cannot but prosper!" cried Cesare, with a look of intense admiration in his handsome eyes.

"Guardian angels cannot do much good unless mortals will be obedient to their. inspirations!" said the Marchesa, with a very bewitching smile, and rising from her seat as she spoke. "But I have no doubt that we shall work to good purpose together, my dear Cesare; and I am very glad to have made the acquaintance of the unknown cousin, of whom I had heard so much," she added, as she gave him her hand—a long, white, cold, slender hand, with long tapering fingers, which somehow or other, as he took it in his, provokingly contrasted itself in his mind with the little brown, warm hand which he had so often held in his in the days separated from the present only by some fifty or sixty hours, and as many miles!

"To me, signora," said he, as he stooped and touched the beautiful hand in his with his lip, " the pleasure of this meeting has been as great as it was unexpected, and —— "

" A good augury, I hope, for our future concord !" she said, interrupting him.   " But now I must leave you to make your confessions and submission, and receive forgiveness from the Marchese.   It is about his time for coming from his chamber.   Remember, now, to take your scolding like a good boy! and to make good promises for the future!   And if the Marchese should seem to be severe, you are not to be vexed or discouraged, or, above all, rebellious.   All will come right; I am there !"

And so with a last nod, and a bright smile, she

glided out of the room, as such women can and do glide out of rooms, leaving Cesare more absorbed in thinking of the interview just over, than in preparing for that to come.

END OF VOL. I.

VIRTUE AND CO., PRINTERS, CITY ROAD, LONDON.

www.ingramcontent.com/pod-product-compliance
Lightning Source LLC
Chambersburg PA
CBHW020849020726
47497CB00005B/1325